ENCOUNT

The picture of the mountain with its glacier gleaming and sinister and the chalet lower down recalled it all so plainly. What an amazing mixture of farce and drama, tragedy and comedy, hostility and love that Austrian holiday had been. Kate would never forget it. She would perhaps in time be vague about Miss Courtland, Monsieur Corbeil, Max Corinth, but some things she would never forget. That moment in time, for instance, when she had sat at the table by the fountain and looked across the courtyard to see Gareth standing there and had felt as though a bomb had exploded beneath her.

**Also by the same author,
and available in Coronet Books:**

**The Tangled Wood
Alex and the Raynhams
A Sheltering Tree
The Family Web
A Magic Place**

Encounter at Alpenrose

Iris Bromige

CORONET BOOKS
Hodder Paperbacks Ltd., London

Copyright © 1970 by Iris Bromige
First published by Hodder & Stoughton Ltd, 1970
Coronet edition 1972
Second impression 1973

The characters in this book are entirely imaginary and bear no relation to any living person

This book is sold subject to the condition that it shall not, by way of trade or otherwise, be lent, re-sold hired out or otherwise circulated without the publisher's prior consent in any form of binding or cover other than that in which this is published and without a similar condition including this condition being imposed on the subsequent purchaser.

Printed in Great Britain for Coronet Books, Hodder Paperbacks Ltd., St. Paul's House, Warwick Lane, London, E.C.4, by Cox & Wyman Ltd., London, Reading and Fakenham

ISBN 0 340 16077 2

CONTENTS

Chapter		page
1	A Snapshot	7
2	Hotel Alpenrose	17
3	First Round	26
4	A Lamb and a Wolf	35
5	Party Tricks	47
6	Close Quarters	60
7	Ann	75
8	Sleight-of-Hand	85
9	Mountain Excursion	98
10	Monsieur Corbeil	107
11	A Little Star-shine	115
12	Visitor from the Past	125
13	Mutual Aid	140
14	Landmark	148
15	Climbing	155
16	A Time to Talk	168
17	Falcon Recaptured	180
18	Postscript	188

1

A Snapshot

I BREATHED a sigh of relief when at last I came clear of the brick and concrete jungle of London and its suburbs and was able to let my little Morris out over the downs, reflecting ruefully that my home, once enjoying rural seclusion, now had a slender green barrier of barely four miles between it and the encroaching urban tide. Bray Hill itself had changed little, though, apart from the increasing number of cars, very much in evidence in the village on that sunny Saturday morning in May. The tree-lined roads looked their best at this time of the year, with hawthorn, cherry and lilac in bloom, and the first fresh green turning the avenue of limes to a translucent tunnel. The chestnut tree with its white candles of flower greeted me like an old friend as I swung round the last corner and drove into the garage drive of the house where I had lived for the first twenty-one years of my life.

Aunt Ella came out of the front door before I had drawn up, flitting across the lawn like a bird on the wing, her small pink face smiling and eager as a child's.

"Kate, dear, how good to see you! Did you have a tiresome journey? I think it's so brave of you to drive a car through that awful London traffic. You look a little tired. In need of some good fresh air, I expect. It seems a long time since we saw you."

"All of six weeks, Aunt Ella," I said, smiling and kissing her, and letting her quick babble of talk waft over me like a welcoming breeze.

My father came out of his study and took both my hands in his.

"Well, Kate," he said, "is fortune still smiling on you?"

"I've no complaints."

"Good."

"Coffee's ready. As it's so warm, we'll have it in the garden. You must be ready for it, dear, after that journey," said Aunt Ella.

I was accustomed to my aunt referring to the twenty-mile journey from London as a major undertaking, but I did feel a little tired and the smell of coffee was inviting. My father was edging back into his study, but Aunt Ella, whose bright blue eyes missed very little, said briskly:

"No finishing *The Times,* Roland. Bad for the coffee, and Kate comes before *The Times.*"

"So she does. I was only going to fetch my pipe. It did occur to me that you two might like a heart-to-heart over the coffee cups, though."

"We can all three have a heart-to-heart over the coffee cups," said Aunt Ella.

My father smiled wryly as his eyes met mine, then he went to fetch his pipe. Anyone less given to heart-to-hearts than my dry, ironical, detached father, I did not know. But he added the pinch of salt to the sweet soufflé mind of my aunt, and I loved them both dearly.

The little garden was bright with tulips and forget-me-nots, pansies and wallflowers, all growing in the sweet confusion favoured, so typically, by my aunt. Not for her beds of this and beds of that. All in together, with scarcely a square inch of bare earth to be seen. I sipped my coffee, listened to my aunt's news of local affairs and felt the tension and urgency of my workaday life begin to slip away from me and relaxation ease in. I had never fully appreciated what we, my father and I, owed to Aunt Ella until I left home and went to work and live in London. She had come to Rowan Cottage to look after us after my mother died when I was seventeen years old. And now, whenever I came back, it was always a pleasure, never a duty, and with a keener appreciation of the happy home she had made for us.

"And now, dear," said Aunt Ella, when I had finished my second cup, "that's enough about our small affairs. Tell us your news. Is the Danville Typing Service still doing well, and are your book sales good? There aren't any copies left in our local bookshops. I always look, of course."

"I doubt whether the position has changed materially since Kate's last report a few weeks ago," said my father.

"We're still just as busy in Victoria Street. We're taking on an extra room in the building next month, and that'll ease the congestion. And my publishers are very pleased with my second book, which will be published in October, and want to know how the third one is getting on," I said.

"And how is it?" asked my father.

"It isn't. I've just torn up what I'd written. It seemed no more than a repetition of the first."

"You're trying to do too much. Run a business and write books," said Aunt Ella.

"I like to be busy," I said, knowing that since I had broken off my engagement to Gareth, I'd never given myself time for reflection. I'd never really stopped running. But I'd got somewhere.

"Not conducive to good writing, being pulled in several directions at once," observed my father.

"I've just come to the same conclusion. That's why I'm thinking of making Joyce my partner in the business, and only holding a watching brief myself in future. And also, wait for it, I'm going to take my first holiday for four years. A whole month, which I'm going to spend in Austria getting material for a new book."

"That's splendid news," said my aunt. "You've been working yourself into the ground. When are you going?"

"The tenth of June. John Castleford has friends who have turned an old house in the Tyrol into a hotel. Sounds just the retreat I want. John's coming for the first week."

"How nice for you," said Aunt Ella, her bright blue eyes regarding me like an enquiring bird. "When he drove you down here last Christmas, I though he was such a reassuring sort of person. I'd hoped we might see more of him."

"What your aunt really means is, are we likely to see more of him in future?" observed my father, lighting his pipe.

"Could be," I said lightly. "Are those lilies-of-the-valley I see blooming over there?"

"Yes," said my aunt triumphantly. "At last I've succeeded with them, after trying them in about ten different places without success."

I lay back in my deck-chair, the sun warm on my face, and listened to my aunt's tale of the triumphs and defeats in the garden which she loved so much. A little breeze brought the may blossom tumbling on to the lawn to lie like confetti under the hawthorn tree. A baby thrush, parked under a forsythia bush, was being fed by its mother, its yellow beak gaping eagerly, its downy speckled feathers toning into the dappled sunshine and shadow beneath the bush. A peaceful enclosed little world, where there were no decisions to be taken, no demands to be met, no clients to consider. Only, perhaps, the odd awkward question to parry, and the sudden jab of memory. The white petals of a hawthorn tree had been scattered on and around me when I had lain on the grass beside Gareth and he had asked me to marry him. A few petals had clung to his thick black hair. That was five years ago, but the sickly sweet scent of may blossom never failed to remind me of that day.

The week-end passed happily. I pottered in the garden, picked gooseberries for the first gooseberry pie on Sunday, and went for a walk over the heath with my father on Sunday afternoon.

"The choice between being a business woman and a writer: is it a hard one?" he asked with characteristic abruptness as we were walking home.

"No. I always wanted to write. You know that. But the business has been surprisingly successful, and I don't want to give it up entirely until I know I can keep myself on what I earn as a writer. But I'm going to sort a few things out during this holiday. Take stock, as it were. Never seem to have time to think about my own personal affairs with a business to run and books I want to write."

"Wasn't that the idea?" asked my father drily.

I smiled and squeezed his arm.

"Yes. And it worked marvellously. I found freedom and independence and the satisfaction of a career that takes all I've got. In fact, I found myself. But now I've reached a stage when I've got to make a choice. Between business and writing. That's not difficult. Just a matter of organising. But also between remaining single and marrying. John has asked me to marry him. In fact, this is the third time of asking. I've promised him my answer after the holiday."

There was silence between us for a few minutes, then my father said:

"I seem to remember some vehement declarations about remaining free and never tying yourself to a man again when you broke with Gareth and left home."

"I was a very raw egg then. And after the mauling Gareth gave me, it was a natural reaction. John's a very different kettle of fish."

"A good deal older than you."

"Ten years. He's been a good friend to me. Helped me with financial advice in the early days of the business, and in dozens of ways besides."

"That early business with Gareth. You've had no regrets?"

"None. Gareth and I were totally unsuited. It would never have worked. He would have swallowed me up, or else it would have been a cat and dog fight all the time. It taught me a lesson, though. And, in a way, set me free. I doubt whether I should have tackled London to make a living and write in my spare time with quite such blazing determination if Gareth hadn't made me feel I had to prove myself. Prove that I was an individual, not his shadow. So perhaps I should feel grateful to him."

"You were very young. Twenty's no age."

"You don't think I was wrong?"

"To avoid the pitfalls and hazards of marriage? Never, my dear," he said with a little smile.

"You think I should continue to avoid them?"

"Who am I to advise my successful daughter? After all, she's built up a flourishing little business from scratch, with no capital and only her own initiative and hard work, and as if that weren't enough, published a book that has had some success. At twenty-five, that's no mean record. I'm only an obscure retired schoolmaster who's spending his dotage trying to learn Greek, a sad gap in my education, I feel. I'm not the one to give advice. I should seek it."

"I'm not pandering to that mock modesty," I said crisply. "I've been lucky. I happened to hit on a business where demand exceeded supply, simply because typing was all I could do. And don't think I have any exalted ideas about my writing. Just light entertainment. And although you never offer advice, I think it worth seeking. Spending so much time with those old Greeks has given you a certain wisdom, perhaps."

"Well, shall we say has taught me to be philosophical? Always easy where other people are concerned, of course."

"You liked Gareth, didn't you?"

"You know my predilection for good brains. That young man had a razor-sharp one. Not necessarily an advantage in a husband."

"So you'd advise me to keep on avoiding the pitfalls and hazards of marriage, would you?"

"My dear Kate, your life is your own and you have proved yourself to be a young woman of great resource and good judgment. I offer no advice to one so well equipped to make her own decisions. It does just occur to me, though, that because you once suffered from a very hard option, you may feel more inclined to go for what appears a soft option. You've made a good and satisfying life for yourself. Be sure, when you change it, that it's for something positively better, not negatively comfortable. That way, you could find yourself in another kind of prison."

"What did you think of John?"

"Very sound. Kind. A little lacking in imagination, perhaps, but a thoroughly nice chap, I'm sure. And in spite of your flattering me by apparently asking my advice, I think you're really just telling me that you mean to say yes this time, and you hope I approve of my future son-in-law."

"Could be," I said, laughing. "But just now, I'm saying nothing definite. Just looking forward to my first holiday for four years and a chance to get a new background for my next book, and plan it in peace."

"A very enjoyable prospect. Are you taking the car?"

"Yes. I'm driving there. John's flying two days later. He's got a directors' meeting he can't miss, but we should arrive on the same day."

For the rest of the way home, we chatted about Austria and my route across Europe. We had tea in the garden until the sound of church bells sent my aunt trotting up the lane to the old greystone church by the village green while I cleared the tea-things. It was a warm, peaceful evening, and a blackbird was trying out some new phrases on the hazel tree outside the kitchen window as I dried Aunt Ella's best tea-set, the one with pink cabbage roses on fine white china. My father was writing letters in his study, and, feeling suddenly restless, I finished clearing up and told him that I was going across to the pond to see the courting antics of the ducks.

"Very salutary, I'm sure," he said, looking at me over his half-moon glasses. "The ducks are always so unwilling, but they get caught in the end."

I sat on the seat by the pond watching the ducks and the moorhens and the swans, just as I had watched them when I was a child. How ordered and well marked the seasons were in the country. The first wood anemones in March; the first green on the hedgerows and birds collecting material for nests; then the crumpled leaves of the chestnut tree bursting from the sticky buds I loved to pick; the distant sound of a cuckoo; baby ducks on the pond, bobbing balls of fluff in their parents' wake; trees heavy in leaf and grasses flowering in the meadow; heather purple on the heath and red admiral and peacock butterflies on michaelmas daisies; autumn leaves and rooks winging home from ploughed fields at dusk; frosty hedgerows and the nightly hoots of owls; and then the first celandines at the foot of the hedgerow, and hazel catkins and pussy willow to pick before the wood anemones came round again. The pattern never varied. There were always the same sights and sounds of the seasons to welcome. Perhaps that was where the country child scored over the town-dweller.

That sense of continuity. During the last four years in London, the seasons had passed by unmarked except by the vagaries of the climate, and I had given myself no time to miss the old calendar.

On an impulse, I walked home through long meadow, a circuitous route and one which I had not taken for years. The footpath crossed it diagonally from stile to stile, through long grass brightened now with buttercups glowing in the oblique rays of the setting sun. The meadow was surrounded by old trees which cast pools of shadow, and in one corner was the leaning hawthorn tree, pushed out of true by its neighbours, stretching out its branches in a semi-circle and shedding its white petals on the grass beneath, just as it had five years ago.

I sat on the stile nearby, a little impatient with this reminiscent mood and yet not able quite to dismiss it. Gareth's name had not been mentioned for years, and lately he had been quite absent from my thoughts. But my father's mention of him today, and the old snapshot which my aunt had produced out of the blue at teatime, had brought that ghost to life again. Aunt Ella had found the snapshot in a book, she said, and did I want it? Her tone of voice and cherubic little face had conveyed nothing more than the kind of casual concern applicable to a thing of no importance but which, since it was mine, she would not throw away without mentioning it. But with Aunt Ella, you never knew.

"Good heavens!" I had exclaimed. "Lord Byron and that wimbly-wambly mess that was me at twenty. No, I don't want that memento of past follies."

"Why not frame it and keep it before you as a warning?" my father had said, and I'd laughed and stuffed the snapshot in my pocket.

I took it out now, and across the years that dark face, full of handsome menace, looked back at me with telling impact even after so long an absence from my life. Not for Gareth the conventional snapshot smile. With a hand resting on my shoulder, he seemed to be regarding the camera with smouldering hostility. I was grinning with idiotic complacency, caught like a spider in the web of his attraction. The snapshot had been taken by my aunt in the garden during the summer of our engagement. What a mess I'd been then, I thought, eyeing the long hair and skimpy cotton dress with a kind of pity. Hopelessly ill-equipped to stand up against the force of Gareth's personality. I had gone down like a ninepin to his first ball, and had remained helpless for a whole year. Crazily in love, I had found myself completely dominated by him. Only at the end had I begun to realise that I no longer had a mind of my own, that he made all the decisions, that I was dwindling into a shadow of Gareth, wishing only to do what he would want, incapable of independent action. He had soon disposed of any little struggle I then made, and I had sometimes wondered whether if it hadn't been for that week-end with Ian Renton and his sister, Janet, which had really hit me where it hurt most, I would ever have broken free and run for my life.

Well, it had all turned out for the best, I thought, as a thrush started up its evening song from the top of a nearby elm. I had escaped, and found myself, and knew my decision had been right. No doubt Gareth now was equally relieved. Perhaps he had found some gentle, clinging girl content to live her life through him, content to be his echo, although really he was not the stuff that husbands should be made of at all; too untamed; taking his own personal freedom for granted as unassailable, and seeing women as pets, at his disposal. After the first few weeks of our break, when I resolutely refused to see him, he had made no effort to find out my whereabouts or get in touch with me again except that when my book was published a year ago, I received a telegram saying "Congratulations. Gareth." I had found it oddly disturbing, and had dithered about acknowledging it. I did not know his address, nor did I wish to know it. At last, I'd telephoned the firm of civil engineers in which he was a partner and been told, to my relief, that he had just returned to Africa on a job there and would be away indefinitely.

Freedom was a lovely thing, I thought, flexing my arms. Looking at that snapshot reminded me what it had done for me, how far I had travelled from that emotion-laden time. And how intense it had all been. I smiled and tore the snapshot into four pieces. It seemed fitting to bury them under the hawthorn tree. I pulled away some turf there and dug a little hole with a sharp-edged stone. With the snapshot interred, I trod the turf down again, amused at my childish fancy.

With the past well and truly buried, I turned my thoughts to the very different Kate Danville of the present as I walked home. With the responsibilities of my business removed from my shoulders for a whole month, I was looking forward tremendously to a relaxed week with John exploring new surroundings and then the pleasure of getting a new book plotted without distraction. John was just the person to put one in a relaxed mood. Always calm, reassuring, ready to co-operate. My father, with his usual shrewdness, had been right. I had all but decided this time to say yes.

2

Hotel Alpenrose

ONE OF THE pleasing rewards of making a modest success of my typing agency had been the purchase of a second-hand car and the freedom it gave me, although learning to drive in London had had its hair-raising moments and I was not a natural driver. Painstaking, was the verdict of my instructor after the first few lessons. However, in the end he had turned me into a competent, careful driver, and I enjoyed my solo journey across Europe to Austria, with the exception of some frightening moments in Paris, when armies of cars seemed to be bearing down on me at high speed, and a feeling of some trepidation when I found myself in competition with Swiss drivers whose panache I could certainly not match.

It was with some relief, however, that I found myself nearing my journey's end on the morning of my third day, for the sun was warm and I was anxious now to be free of the car and to be able to explore on foot. I had left the traffic behind me and the winding road up the valley through pine and larch woods beckoned me on to what I felt sure was going to be the best holiday I had ever had.

John, in his usual efficient way, had drawn me a map. I pulled up and studied it again. This winding road would bring me soon to the village of Mölden. About half a mile beyond, I had to turn up a narrow track on the left which would lead me to the Hotel Alpenrose. It was hot in the car and the trees looked shady and inviting. I fished an apple out of my jumble-bag and sat on a soft carpet of pine needles under the nearest tree to cool off. It was beautifully quiet and peaceful. The empty road twisted ahead between the trees, becoming sparser now, and the only sounds to be heard were the bright little songs of some warblers and the occasional rustle of the trees when the breeze stirred them. I leaned against the trunk of the tree and was happily biting into my apple when the peace I was so much enjoying was shattered by the blare of the horn of a grey car, travelling fast. It only just had room to clear my Morris but did not slacken speed, and had disappeared round the next bend before I had progressed further with my apple. Too fast, I said to myself darkly, and anyway there was no need to make that row, even if I had left the offside door of my car a little ajar and had not parked it quite as far into the bank as I might. John was due to arrive at lunch-time by hired car from Innsbruck, but that had not looked like a hired car, and I hadn't noticed a passenger although it had flashed past me so rapidly that there had been little chance to see inside.

I finished my apple and returned to the car. Soon the valley widened, the woods receded and ahead of me in a green basin between the neighbouring hills, with higher mountains ahead, lay the village of Mölden: white-washed houses, red-roofed, a small white church with a tall red steeple, one fairly large hotel, an inn and a cluster of shops. I noticed the grey car that had passed me parked outside the inn. It was a Mercedes. A narrow river ran through the village spanned by two wooden bridges taking the road first one side of it, then the other. I could not miss the narrow track I had to take beyond the village, for a white board was nailed to the trunk of a larch tree at the junction bearing the words Hotel Alpenrose in large black letters above an arrow pointing up the track. This climbed for a few hundred yards beside a fast-running stream and then swung round to a solid grey stone house set on a grassy plateau between the woods below and hills and mountains behind. I had arrived.

I was warmly welcomed by Frank Easher, the owner, and introduced to his Austrian wife, Elsa.

"John hasn't arrived yet," he said, after we had exchanged greetings. "We're both looking forward to seeing him again. The first time since we left England six years ago."

They were a pleasant couple: Mr Easher was tall, burly and genial-looking with a military bearing, and his wife was fair with blue eyes and regular features. They were both, I judged, in their forties.

"John told us that you would be working on a book," said Mrs Easher in perfect English, with no trace of an accent. "We have put a writing table and chair in your room, and you will find it comfortable, I hope."

I thanked her, signed the visitors' book and was conducted to my room by Franz, the porter. It was the last one along the corridor, a large, airy room, as clean as a new pin, and it looked out on to a delightful courtyard below. I had not realised that the house was L-shaped. The bedrooms were in one branch, the public rooms, kitchen and staff quarters in the other, and the courtyard between the two was gravelled. A mountain ash tree grew on the far side. Brightly painted tables and chairs were set at intervals there, and an ornamental well-head beneath my window bore a crown of geraniums and marguerites on its wrought-iron frame. The same flowers were used in the window-boxes outside the rooms overlooking the courtyard, and repeated in an oval bed in the centre of the courtyard itself. There were two wrought-iron lanterns on each wall, and a small fountain played in one corner. The whole effect was charming on that day of brilliant sunshine which enhanced the colours of the flowers and made the fountain sparkle, while the breeze was just strong enough to make a flickering pattern of sunshine and shadow beneath the mountain ash tree. As I stood by the window enjoying it, I reflected that John could not have recommended a place to please me better.

I had washed and was just finishing unpacking when there was a knock on the door and Franz informed me that Mr Castleford had just arrived and would meet me in the courtyard for a drink in ten minutes' time.

I chose the table nearest the fountain for the pleasure of hearing the cool splash of the water. The only other person there was a middle-aged man of stolid build who was sitting at a table close to the well-head reading a paper, a half empty brandy glass beside him. John joined me a few moments later.

"Good journey?" he asked, and I told him about it and said how much I liked the hotel.

"I thought you would. Sound chap, Frank Easher. Used to play a good game of golf. Don't suppose he has much opportunity now."

I sipped my glass of iced lager and felt as contented as a cat in the sun. John was talking about the bank rate and my glass was half-way to my lips when I saw a lean, dark man surveying me from the hotel porch, glass in hand, and the world seemed to stop with a violent jerk. It wasn't possible. A trick of the light. I stared, transfixed, thinking I must be mistaken. But there was no mistaking that black hair and wide forehead, or the brooding intensity of the dark eyes beneath those heavy black brows. Gareth Ferrion. The last person I wanted to see. I could not have felt more shaken if a bomb had exploded. I had spilt some beer on my linen skirt and my hand trembled as I put the glass down on the table.

"Here," said John, offering the handkerchief from his breast pocket. "I say, are you all right? You look pale."

"Felt a bit giddy for a moment. Been driving too much. You know how it is. You feel you're still moving. I won't mess your handkerchief up, John. Mine will cope."

"Sure you're all right?" he said again after I'd mopped up.

"Absolutely. Never better. I can't wait to explore this lovely country, and my notebook's at the ready," I said quickly.

It seemed as though Gareth hadn't seen me, after all, for he walked to a table behind us with no sign of recognition. I was half in the shade and he had probably been looking past me. I was angry and bewildered by the force of his impact on me. All that was over years ago. I was a different person now. Why on earth was I behaving like a frightened mouse? There was nothing sinister about Gareth. No reason to feel anything more than the usual surprise felt when one encountered an old acquaintance in a place remote from one's usual environment. I began to talk to John about my plans for the week we were to spend together with a degree of enthusiasm which surprised him, for he said with a smile:

"I've never seen you excited before. The cool, efficient young head of the Danville Typing Service has become air-borne."

Not air-borne, I thought. Just fighting for air. I stopped babbling and listened to John on the subject of exchange rates with every appearance of absorption while I tried to collect myself. When the tap on my shoulder came some minutes later, I was more or less ready for it.

"Hullo, Kate," he said, standing beside me and looking at me with a searching expression.

I stared up, blinking, feigning bewilderment for a moment.

"I'm sorry . . ." I murmured, then allowed a smile to come to my lips. "Why, it's Gareth . . . Gareth Ferrion, isn't it?"

His expression had changed to one of sardonic smoothness.

"Right first time," he said.

"How extraordinary! Meeting you here, after all these years. John, may I introduce Gareth Ferrion? He was a friend and neighbour of ours once. John Castleford."

The two men shook hands and John, to my annoyance, asked Gareth to join us, which he did with a gleam in his eyes that I recognised. Well, it was an opportunity to put things on the right footing straight away, and I took it, goaded by a panic-stricken little demon inside me.

"I'm surprised that you recognised me," I said with a polite smile. "I was little more than a child when we last saw each other."

"I have a good memory for faces," he replied blandly.

"And where are you living now?"

"Temporarily in a rented flat in Kensington. I've been abroad for the last two years. And you?"

"In London. I go home quite often at the week-end. They'll be very surprised to learn that I've run across you here."

"It's a small world," he said wickedly, and I hastily slid my eyes from him and studied the ornamental well-head, not wishing to betray the fact that I would like to push him down it.

"Abroad? Where was that?" asked John politely.

"Africa. Working on the construction of a dam."

John enquired further, and on learning the name of Gareth's firm of consulting civil engineers, claimed acquaintance with a partner now retired.

"Only a slight acquaintance," he explained. "A question of finance some years ago. Interesting work, yours. What are conditions like now in that part of Africa?"

Before long they were deep in a discussion of the financial problems of the African states while I looked around me, inwardly seething, outwardly not interested, until John said:

"We're boring Kate with these economics. Not that she isn't a good business woman herself at home, but she's in a holiday mood now and wants to forget all bread and butter matters."

"So you're a good business woman now, are you, Kate? You must have changed. She was a naïve, impractical young thing when I knew her," said Gareth to John.

"Naïve? Impractical? Kate? I can't believe it," said John, half smiling.

"People grow up," I said calmly.

"Well, I can tell you she's a very successful, efficient business woman now, and a writer. Did you know?" added John.

"Only one book to my credit," I broke in quickly. "And light weight, at that."

"You're too modest," said John. "Not that I wouldn't put your business achievement first. To have built that up without any capital to start with is quite something. Nice to have a hobby that gives people as much enjoyment as your writing does, though."

I wriggled my toes. There was no reason to feel prickly whenever John referred to my writing as a hobby, which he frequently did. But to me, writing was my life blood, all I had ever wanted to do, and involved toil and sweat and tears and intense concentration. If I ever earned enough by writing to keep myself, I should retire from the Danville Typing Service without a pang, although with a sense of gratification at having been able to make a living for myself while I learned to write something saleable. I did not like the personal tone of this conversation. Gareth was taking a malicious enjoyment in it, I knew.

"Are you staying here for long, Gareth?" I asked politely.

"A few weeks. And you?"

I tried to hide my dismay, for I had hoped he might just have been passing through, and said shortly:

"For a month. I plan to work on a new book."

"A very pleasant place to work in."

"Yes, isn't it? Off the beaten track. How did you come to hear of it?"

"Through a friend," said Gareth calmly, giving away absolutely nothing.

"How long have you been here?"

"I only arrived this morning."

John began to talk about Frank Easher and his wife, explaining to Gareth how they had inherited the house on the death of Elsa's parents and had decided to turn it into a hotel. There seemed to be no way of cutting this encounter short. John, sociable and expansive, seemed set for another hour and Gareth sat there looking indolent but with those dark grey eyes of his as alert as a hawk's, missing nothing. The two men could not have been more dissimilar, I mused, letting the conversation pass over me.

John, verging on the portly, with his blunt-featured, affable face, had suggested to me when I first met him a very nice public school headmaster. He was, in fact, a director in a firm of merchant bankers, where his air of genial confidence was no doubt equally valuable. I knew of nobody who could so quickly allay anxiety, dispel worry, as John. In the early, struggling days of my business he had been the greatest help. His light brown hair was thinning a little on top, although he was only in his mid-thirties, but with his fair complexion and good teeth, he gave an impression of excellent health, meticulous grooming, and good, conventional tailoring.

Beside him, Gareth looked more saturnine than ever. A little above average height, without an ounce of spare flesh on him, his usually brown complexion had a sallow tinge now and there were shadows under the grey eyes that were so dark that sometimes they looked black. He moved with the loose-limbed ease of the natural athlete, and even now, lounging back in the chair, there was a lithe grace about him, as though at the drop of a hat he could be on his toes, alert for anything. It had always been part of his striking personality, this air of lazy grace coupled with a contradictory smouldering intensity which perhaps came from the

Celtic strain in him, for his mother had been Welsh. He could be as infectiously gay as a sunny May morning, as menacing as a July storm, and as biting as an icy January morning, I thought, indulging my weakness for literary similes. And I had been madly in love with him, dominated by him, frightened of him and angry with him. And in the end, I'd escaped by the skin of my teeth to find myself. And I was never, never going to get into that mad emotional state again when my mind was no longer my own.

I stood up, gave the men a friendly smile and excused myself on the plea of completing my unpacking. In my bedroom, I sat on the bed and took stock of this unexpected situation which threatened the peace I had so much looked forward to. During the intense activity of the past four years, I had pushed Gareth out of my thoughts for ever, I had believed. I was content with my life, confident as I had never been before, delighted to have had a book published and to have a chance now to make a career of writing. Gareth had nothing to do with that life, and I was amazed and disturbed by the fact that I had not reacted to this unexpected encounter with the detachment which I had attained towards the mental image of him. In my thoughts he had become that forceful young man who had bowled me over when I was little more than a child, and I viewed both protagonists in that episode with the kind of wry amusement which one felt when viewing old snapshots. Had we really looked like that? Didn't we realise how odd we looked? But at the first sight of him an hour ago, where was that amused detachment? Had I been kidding myself all these years?

I pulled myself together. This was ridiculous. Perhaps I was more tired by the driving than I had realised. There was nothing in the present situation that need disturb me. A slight embarrassment at this unexpected reminder of past foolishness, no more. With a stern admonishment to myself to play it cool, I unfolded one of the maps I had brought with me and studied it with a view to deciding which way to explore that afternoon.

After I had worked it out, I went to the window and glanced down at the courtyard below. John and Gareth were still talking. The solitary man I had first seen had gone, but with lunch-time approaching, more guests had appeared. A smart, fair-haired woman in a trim blue linen dress and white sandals was sitting at a table by herself ferreting inside a large and expensive-looking white bag. Immediately below my window was a woman with a girl of about eighteen and a boy a few years younger: the girl looked unhappy; the boy was talking eagerly. At the table nearest the hotel entrance sat a fair-haired, big-framed man with a whisky glass in front of him. He was wearing a rather stunning scarlet silk shirt over a pair of pale grey drill trousers, and he gave an expansive grin and lifted his hand as two sunburnt young men in shorts appeared in the doorway. They smiled and accepted the invitation to join him. I almost overlooked a grey-haired little woman sitting in the deepest shade of the mountain ash tree reading a book, a coffee cup beside her.

As I lingered there, avoiding looking at John and Gareth, I played the old guessing game. I placed the well-groomed fair woman as an American career woman and thought her a shade sophisticated for this kind of country hotel. The woman and two children below me I placed as a middle-class English family, but the fair man in the scarlet shirt had me completely foxed. A film star? Or perhaps a television personality? The two young men in shorts with their fair hair and sturdy good looks I was sure were Austrians. The shadowy lady in her pale summer frock was too nearly invisible to be able to make any guess about her. I was probably miles out in my guesses, anyway. Only two Austrians out of the ten people visible to me seemed unlikely. We were, after all, in Austria. Perhaps the eleventh person, the stolid, middle-aged man who had left the courtyard, was Austrian, but as I recollected his swarthy complexion and far from handsome features, I doubted it. Counting myself, I mused, we numbered twelve.

I broke off my cogitations as a bell rang for lunch, and, feeling that I now had myself well in hand after that astonishing cavorting at the sight of Gareth, I went down the wide wooden staircase to the dining-room, reminding myself with pleasurable anticipation that this was the real beginning of my first holiday for years, and no ghosts were going to disturb it.

3

First Round

I SOON DISCOVERED that I must either curb my liking for exploring on foot or else leave John to his own devices, for walking was not his idea of enjoyment and he regarded my enthusiasm with indulgent amusement. He thought walking had gone out when cars came in, and although he submitted on the first afternoon, when I dragged him up a winding path to a track half-way up a mountain, it was obvious that he was not enjoying it. I had planned to follow the mountain track, but John sat down on a wooden bench outside the refreshment hut at the beginning of the track as though we had achieved our goal at great cost, and any thought of going farther was mere folly.

He sat there mopping his brow while I fetched some cold drinks. He would have done better, I thought, if he had discarded his conventional tweed jacket and collar and tie for an open sports shirt and had worn some canvas shoes instead of the brown leather ones, which had started off shining like a chestnut but were now coated with grey dust.

We sipped our drinks and John told me about the man who had sat next to him in the aeroplane. He was the director of an insurance company. I listened with a fraction of my attention, the rest being fixed on the track ahead which wound along half-way up the mountain side, through heather and whortleberry bushes and the little wild rhododendrons which gave our hotel its name. I could see a stream crossing the track, flashing white over the boulders. Beyond the foothills surrounding us were the high mountains crowned with snow against the blue backdrop of the sky. The track beckoned me enticingly and I couldn't think of a less suitable subject to be talking about than insurance.

It seemed unsociable to leave John on that first day and continue along the track on my own, so we lingered at the hut, then sauntered slowly back through the pine woods to the hotel, where we had tea in the courtyard on our own. After tea, we drove into Innsbruck, and John was able to buy *The Times*.

I dressed with care that evening, anxious to present the cool, mature Kate Danville to Gareth's eyes. When I was ready, I studied myself in the mirror with an intent gaze that suggested that I was as anxious to convince myself that there was no connection between the present and the past as I was to convince Gareth. Instead of the long windblown chestnut hair and eager smile of that girl in the snapshot I saw a serious face and ear-length hair taken back from the forehead and curving nicely round at the temples, a tribute to my hairdresser's skill with scissors for my thick hair was self-willed. Dark brown eyes, straight nose, wide mouth. Not much colour as yet, and decidedly thinner. The plain, sleeveless lime green dress was far removed, too, from the shapeless little cotton frock of the snapshot. I gave myself a wry grin. I felt reasonably well armoured. And why should I think that Gareth cared two hoots, anyway, how I looked now? That first searching look had doubtless satisfied any curiosity he may have felt. Now we could meet like civilised acquaintances.

Gareth sat at a corner table in the dining-room, and as luck would have it, our table was next to his. I gave him the kind of pleasant smile and "Good evening" which I would give to my business associates, and he replied with a sardonic lift of his heavy black eyebrows and a smile I didn't much care for. John was pulling out the chair which would have me facing in Gareth's direction, and I quickly ignored it and sat down with my back to Gareth. I wanted to enjoy my meals.

It was a warm evening and we had coffee out in the courtyard. When John suggested that we might invite my friend to join us, I snapped:

"No. If you don't mind," I added more gently. "I'd rather not get involved."

"Just as you like, my dear. An interesting chap, I thought."

We sat there, chatting. I found it something of an effort. Out of our London setting, John and I seemed a bit astray with one another. Or perhaps it was just me, for when I suggested a stroll, John said:

"You seem a bit nervy, Kate. I think that journey must have tired you. You should have flown out."

"Not nervy. I just feel rather excited at being free of all commitments and with this lovely country to explore after being caged in London."

He smiled indulgently.

"You're like a child over this holiday. After a few weeks, you'll be looking forward to getting back to your commitments, as you call them. That's your sphere, Kate. You're a business woman."

"Am I?" For a brief, bewildering moment I felt as if I didn't know who or what I was.

"Of course. A most proficient one, too. I admire that calm competence of yours more than I can say. But you know that."

I wouldn't have thought those were particularly lovable qualitics, and I wondered not for the first time why John wanted to marry me. I had a sudden uneasy feeling that he didn't know me at all.

"What about that stroll?" I said.

"Well, if you don't mind, my dear, I'm expecting a telephone call this evening. At least, I said I'd be here if Rankin wanted to consult me on a certain matter that's coming to the boil sooner than expected. But don't let me stop you," he added politely.

"Oh no, it doesn't matter. It's very pleasant here."

The fair woman had just joined Gareth at the table by the fountain. Her voice in the dining-room had confirmed my guess about her nationality. She was wearing a black sleeveless dress and looked as polished and expensive as the diamond clip on her shoulder. And I thought again that she looked a little out of place in this small country hotel; Nice or Cannes or Nassau would seem more suitable backgrounds. Gareth was smiling as he leaned forward to light her cigarette. The light twill jacket he wore emphasised his dark colouring; his years in Africa had made him leaner than ever, emphasising the bonework of forehead and jaw.

"You don't say, Mr Ferrion. Well, now, that *is* interesting."

The nasal American voice wafted clearly to us on that calm evening. Gareth's deep voice was quite indistinguishable. I brought my attention back to John, who was talking about the need to expand my business premises.

"You're terribly cramped there, Kate. I think you should accept that offer of all three rooms on the next floor instead of just the one."

"Oh, I don't know. I'm thinking of taking a back seat and handing over most of the responsibility to Joyce Burland. I want to concentrate on writing."

"But my dear girl, isn't that premature? Delegate more by all means, but keep the reins in your hands. Joyce isn't your size. You could build that business up into a really big enterprise. You surely won't be satisfied to take a back seat now that it's doing so well."

"But I was never interested in building up a big enterprise, John. Or even a small one. It somehow happened. I only wanted to earn my living while I tried to write a book and get it published."

"But you'll still have your spare time for any writing."

"I want to give it all my time and energy."

"Don't let it turn your head, my dear, having a book published. It may seem glamorous but it's unlikely to earn you much money and writing is a very hazardous career. I don't think that business will be the same without you running it, and it would be a pity to see it decline after all your work."

"You know I don't want to lose my freedom, John, but if we married, would you really want the dregs of me after an exacting business as well as writing had taken their toll?"

"Don't try to tell me that you're a cosy little stay-at-home woman after all, Kate. I have what you call the dregs of you now. I find them very pleasant. My housekeeper is efficient and will give you a much easier time than you have now, when you have to look after a flat and do your own chores. You won't have to do a thing, except play hostess when we entertain. You'd be bored stiff without the Danville Typing Service, and writing wouldn't suffice. A lonely job, no contacts. Keep it as a hobby, by all means. But to give up your business would be most foolish, believe me. I think you're a bit tired just now. You should take more holidays, delegate a bit more."

He was so rational always. If I was the person he thought I was, he would be dead right. Perhaps I was. Caught just now between past and present, I didn't really know.

"I'll think about it," I said.

He patted my arm.

"You do that. I know you, Kate. If you'll marry me, you won't lose your freedom. We'll both have our own business spheres. No tiresome demands on each other. It's because women have empty lives at home that they make demands on men and are possessive, and then the trouble starts. You and I aren't like that. We've absorbing lives of our own. We can make our marriage a very pleasant partnership. I know you don't like emotional involvement any more than I do. We're made for each other, you know."

I looked at the future through John's eyes. A wife who would make no demands, who would earn her own keep and have an absorbing job that would leave him without distraction from his own work. We would come together at the end of the day, exchange news, dine well in a house smoothly tailored to his comfort by a housekeeper he had had for years. What would we bring each other? I could see that it would be an advantage for John to have a wife to act as hostess, for he had a wide range of business friends. There would be companionship for what little spare time we had, and perhaps more spare time together would put a strain on it. A cool marriage, successful, perhaps, within its limits. No heights. No depths. But comfortable.

I was spared the necessity of replying to John's statement by the arrival of Franz to say that there was a telephone call from London for Mr Castleford.

"I think I'll fetch my coat and have a short stroll, John, while you attend to business."

"Righto, my dear. I may have a few calculations to make and a letter to write afterwards, so I'll see you at breakfast. Sleep well."

He walked across the courtyard, unhurried as always, and disappeared into the hotel.

It was growing dark as I left the hotel to take the path up the hill. I had to pass the shady enclosure where the cars were parked and I noticed the grey Mercedes that had disturbed my peace that morning. The footpath kept beside the twisting stream, which ran even faster here than it had below the hotel, tumbling over and round huge boulders, between banks of grass and ferns and patches of flowers which I could not identify in the fading light, but guessed to be saxifrages. I sat on a boulder and listened to the sound of the water as the first stars appeared and a ghostly light behind a distant snowy peak gave notice of the rising moon. I waited until it came clear of the mountain, casting its cool silvery light over the whole range and giving added sparkle to the stream rushing past me.

It was such a beautiful night that it seemed a pity to return to the hotel, but my shoes were wet with dew and unsuitable for further exploration. And, moreover, I was suddenly aware that I was tired after the exciting activities of the past few days. The country would wait for me. I had four whole weeks. The thought of bed was enticing, but before it claimed me I wanted to add some more notes to the four pages already full in my new notebook.

I turned back, and as I rounded a bend, saw a dark shape ahead of me, standing by the stream looking across at the mountains. A cigarette glowed red. I recognised the silhouette instantly, although he was some way ahead. Something in the set of his shoulders, in his stance, I would always know. My heart quickened, but I reminded myself that we were now just two acquaintances by chance staying at the same hotel. I had the advantage of him because he hadn't seen me, being intent on the mountain.

"Good evening," I said pleasantly as I walked by.

He was beside me, his voice rough with anger.

"How long are you going to keep up this silly game, Kate?"

"What silly game?"

"Pretending not to remember my name. The cool hand-off as though we're strangers."

"But we are now. Embarrassing to both of us, surely, to recall past foolishness."

"I am not easily embarrassed. You used to be honest."

"I am now when I say that we are strangers, and that I don't want to be reminded of the past. For me, it's dead. And for you too, surely, after all this time."

"Strangers? Poppycock, and you know it. When you first saw me today you looked like a petrified rabbit. What are you frightened of? I don't bite."

So he had seen me straight away. I might have known.

"I came here for a peaceful holiday and to do some work on a book. I don't want any distractions."

"Am I a distraction?"

"You always were," I said coldly. "I feared you might be again."

"That's better. I understand your point of view. Just don't turn on the strangers' act, that's all. You and I know each other intimately, my girl, and you can't undo that. I will try, however, not to be a distraction."

I felt my coldness slipping at the old sense of being manipulated. I'm Kate Danville, author and head of a business, I reminded myself fiercely. I have an identity of my own. As I said nothing, he went on in a level tone:

"I was pleased about the book. I knew how much it would mean to you."

"It was kind of you to send the telegram. I tried to get you at your office to thank you but you were abroad."

"I've been out of the country for the past two years, except for one flying visit."

"And now you're taking a month's holiday?"

"M'm. The job in Africa's finished, and I caught a bug out there that left me a bit jaded, so a month off seemed a good idea."

"How did you hit on this place?"

"Recommended by a friend," he said, smooth as silk.

"I like it here. Ideal for working on a book."

"Yes, indeed. Is this the second?"

"No, the third. The second's with my publishers and is due out next October."

"Are you going on with the same kind of book as the first?"

"My publishers want me to, and I guess light entertainment is about my mark. Small beer, I know, but ambitions have to be tailored to capabilities."

"What's wrong with entertainment? I rather like romance added to my thrillers," he said wickedly.

"You've read *Dark Journey*, then?"

"Naturally. Well written. Enjoyable. Your subsidiary characters were cut out of cardboard, though."

Before I could remind myself again that I had no intention of getting involved at any level, we were deep in a discussion of characterisation and the weakness of my minor characters. He knew what he was talking about, and so did I, and I appreciated his honesty and his interest. Afterwards, I wondered whether this was his cunning ploy to break down my guard. Anyway, he succeeded, for by the time we reached the hotel, there was no further pretence that we were strangers. Belatedly, however, I did clutch at the shreds of my protective cloak as we walked upstairs to our rooms.

"Good-night. I'll remember the points you made when I'm writing the next book. Most interesting."

I sounded like a schoolmistress and I saw Gareth's lips twitch.

"I enjoyed the discussion, too. We must talk together again some time, about other things," he said with a look in his eyes which made me slide hastily into the haven of my room. Gareth's was opposite.

I sat on the bed, confused, trying to make sense of it all. Where was I now? In the end I decided firmly that there was nothing to worry about. Total strangers we could not be, and it had been foolish of me to try to establish that, but I had changed a lot since I had broken with Gareth and left home, and four years had made some subtle change in him, too, which was difficult to pinpoint but which made him as slippery as an eel to handle. And that job in Africa must have been a taxing one, for he looked older than his thirty-one years. No reason to think that the past had any relevance for either of us now. I had my book, and John, to concentrate on. When Gareth could not be avoided, I must cling to the cool impersonal touch.

I took out my notebook, and with a considerable effort of will began to jot down notes on the surrounding country which was to be the background of my third book.

4

A Lamb and a Wolf

"THAT TELEPHONE CALL means I'll be busy this morning, Kate. No need to apologise for leaving you on your own, because I know you're longing to go striding over those hills. Perhaps this afternoon you'd like to drive into the mountain range to the south of us," said John as I poured the coffee.

"Good idea. The weather looks favourable."

Gareth had evidently breakfasted early for his table was now being cleared. John preferred to start the day at a more leisurely pace.

I set off from the hotel immediately after breakfast to continue my walk along the footpath I had used the previous night. I felt rested and keen, with a sneaking regret that I had only the morning to spare for a walk which obviously led into the hills for a considerable distance, for I could see the track winding away up the valley. The sun was warm and I did not hurry, stopping to examine the wild flowers and the enormous gaily-coloured grasshoppers which crossed my tracks from time to time. The only people I saw were two small boys with baskets of wood on their backs who gave me a cheerful grin and a *"Grüss Gott"* as they passed.

I marked a small wooded hump as my turning point, and when I reached it, clambered down to the stream about twenty feet below to rest for a few minutes before going back. I was dabbling my fingers in the water, which was icy, when I thought I heard someone sobbing. I put it down to the sound of the water, but then I heard it again, coming from my left. I climbed over some boulders and there, hunched up by the water's edge, was a fair girl in a pink cotton frock and blue cardigan. She didn't see me at first, but when she did she turned quickly away, furtively scrubbing her eyes with her handkerchief. I recognised the straw-coloured hair and plain features as belonging to the girl of the family of three at the hotel. Perhaps it would have been more tactful to have said "Hullo" and have passed on, but there was something so pathetic about that awkward crumpled figure that I went across to her and said:

"What's the trouble? Can I help?"

Her eyes were red and swollen but she made a pathetic effort to hide her distress as she said in a wavering voice:

"N-n-nothing, thanks. Just a bit under the weather."

"On such a lovely morning, on holiday?"

"I know. It just sort of swept over me. The contrast, I mean."

I hesitated. I didn't want to intrude, but there was a lost-puppy appeal about her that made me think that my company would not be unwelcome.

"I want a short rest before I go back to the hotel. Can I join you?"

She sniffed and nodded with a watery smile.

"You must have started early this morning because I didn't see you ahead," I went on.

"I skipped breakfast. There was a row. I didn't want anything to eat."

"Family troubles?"

"Yes. I didn't want to come away with them in the first place. I knew they didn't want me. At least, my mother didn't. And Roger doesn't care whether I'm here or not except that he gets bored with it all."

"Meaning?"

"Oh, the way Mother's always criticising me, and the state I get into. I know I'm a fool. But I can't seem to help it. The more she criticises me and makes fun of me, the worse I am, and then she says I should try to cultivate a sense of humour."

Perhaps because I had suffered from over much criticism from my mother and had been saddled with a vast inferiority complex as a result, I was more sympathetic than I might have been with this abject display of self-pity.

"How old are you?"

"Eighteen last week."

"At school?"

"I left at the end of last term. We're returning to England after this holiday. We've been living in France for the past three years. My father was attached to the British Embassy there. He's been moved back to England now, but he's living in a hotel in London and we're spending a holiday here until our new home is ready for us in three weeks' time."

"And where is your new home?"

"In Hampstead."

"Well, cheer up. Family life may be difficult, but you'll be able to get a job and be independent soon."

"I wanted to go back with my father, but she wouldn't have that. She's my stepmother. Roger is my half-brother. He's all right. At fifteen, you can't expect much," she added with an ingenuous gravity which was touching.

"You get on well with your father, I take it."

"Yes, but not as well as we used to. Oh, I can understand them. I must be an awful disappointment. Not exactly ornamental, no talent, not able to mix."

"Snap out of it," I said briskly. "Get a job and be independent. You'll find your own value then. Stop caring so much about what other people think of you. Any idea what you want to do? You want to earn a living?"

"Of course. I'm going to a secretarial training college when we get back home, but Mother isn't hopeful that I'll benefit."

"Then you'd better surprise her." I glanced at my watch. "Are you going back to the hotel for lunch?"

"I suppose so."

"Then I think we must be moving."

She scrambled to her feet, smoothing with her hand her short straight hair, straightening her crumpled frock. Her face was reddened with the sun, and her pale blue eyes still looked red and sore. With too prominent teeth and a gawky manner, she was indeed far from prepossessing, and crippled as she was by a complete lack of confidence in herself, the outlook was not rosy. But there was something about her honest simplicity that appealed to me and one would have to be very hard-hearted not to want to help such a lame duck.

"I'm sorry I've talked so much about my troubles. So dreary for you," she said shyly as we started to walk back. "Where do you live?"

I told her, and then went on to describe how the Danville Typing Service had come into being, thinking it might encourage her.

"My personal life had come to grief, and like you, I had no special training, except that I could type. I started off in two rooms in London and used one of them as an office for what I termed the Danville Typing Service, which was really me and one old portable typewriter. I put advertisements in literary journals and sent circular letters offering my services to hotels and colleges and anywhere I could think of where there might be people wanting some typing done. To my amazement, I found myself as busy as a beaver. And it grew from that. And believe me, the one sure salvation if you're unhappy is to be so busy that you don't have time to think about it. And if you make a go of your job, self-confidence grows, and that helps enormously. I recommend the treatment."

"Yes, but you're so . . . different."

"I was as uncertain of myself when I left home as you are now. I'm not saying it's easy. A sort of desperate determination is called for. Anyway, you don't want a lecture from me. But you do your best at that secretarial college. And if you want any advice or help, you can get in touch with me. You might fancy starting as a typist with us. Mainly literary work, but varied enough."

"Thank you. Thank you very much," she breathed, her eyes shining with a gratitude that made me wonder whether anybody had ever put themselves out in the slightest degree for this child.

I scribbled my private address and business address on the back page of my notebook, tore it out and gave it to her.

"Either of those will find me."

"You're very kind. I'll put it away safely. My name's Ann. Ann Binlay."

"Have you done much exploring since you've been here, Ann?"

She told me where she had been, and during our walk back to the hotel I gathered that solitary walking was her only refuge. She was interested in wild flowers and wanted to find some edelweiss before she left. We stopped to study some of the flowers on our way back and identified two from a book she had bought in Innsbruck. By the time we got back, she was looking a good deal happier, and the smile she gave me when we parted had a quality that transformed her plain face.

I drove John to the mountains that afternoon, and had my first experience of driving over high Alpine passes. Manipulating countless hair-pin bends took all my concentration, and I had one or two anxious moments. I drew off the road at one viewpoint, thrilled with the panorama around us. A whole range of the high Austrian Alps lay before us, their white contours beautifully shaped against the blue sky. John was faintly amused at my enthusiasm.

"What a temperate man you are, John!" I exclaimed after my exalted wonder at this beauty had evoked a rather absent-minded response.

He smiled and put his hand on my shoulder.

"I've seen it all before, remember."

"But each time, surely, it's just as breath-taking."

"You look attractive in this starry-eyed mood, Kate. I've not seen you like it before."

"There's a track down to that hut by the glacier. I'd like to see a glacier at close quarters. Shall we go?'

"It's a bit rough. Haven't really got the right foot gear. You go if you'd like to, my dear."

"All right. Shan't be long."

I scrambled down the track to the hut which was close to the foot of the enormous glacier which ploughed its way down between jagged rock faces to end in the dirty grey rubble of the moraine. The glacier was an awesome sight, horribly toothed, with jagged ice cliffs and deep crevasses, white and blue in the middle, grey at the moraine edges. Down the bare rock cliffs which contained it, lines of water glistened, snake-like, and the whole effect was both powerful and daunting. Above the glacier lay the smooth snowfields, shining in the sun with a blinding light. Three climbers, roped, were crossing the glacier high up, looking like toy figures. I shivered. Although the snowfields and peaks seemed to offer a splendid challenge, I should hate to cross that glacier, and feared that I was not the stuff that climbers are made of in spite of the fact that my final quarrel with Gareth had been sparked off by just that topic.

"Hullo there," said a cheerful voice, startling me.

I turned to see the fair-haired charmer from the hotel. He was wearing a sheep-skin jacket over fawn trousers and reminded me of a television commercial for sporty cars. If the sheep-skin jacket was overdoing it, my own thin frock and cardigan were rather inadequate against the chilly air of that high altitude.

"Hullo. Breath-taking, isn't it?" I said.

"Kind of dwarfing."

He had a pleasant voice with a faint American drawl. He really was rather an attractive giant, I thought, with his thick fair hair, blue eyes, strong features and magnificent teeth. He had a friendly, lively manner which was disarming.

"I've never been to the Alps before so I'm finding all this most thrilling," I said.

"The first time's always best. A good setting for a book."

I looked at him quickly, and he smiled down at me as he went on:

"Our good proprietor happened to mention that you were Kate Danville, the writer. I hope you don't mind."

"To say 'the writer' is putting it a bit high. I have only one book to my credit so far, and that hasn't made me exactly famous."

"I've heard of it. Now I shall certainly buy it."

"More likely to appeal to women."

"My range is wide. Nice little hotel, the Alpenrose. Needs more private bathrooms. Otherwise, I can't fault it, and I've stayed in a few in my time. Private bathrooms are almost taken for granted at home, of course."

"Home being the United States?"

"My adopted home, perhaps I should say. I've lived in America since I was twenty. But I was born in Kent."

We had begun to climb back to the road.

"By the way," he said, "the number plate's loose on the back of your Morris. Better get it fixed. You might lose it."

"Thanks. I hadn't noticed."

His large American car was parked behind mine. Before we parted, he offered to lend me what he said was a very good guide to the district. He'd look it out for me, he said, and caught me by surprise with a quick squeeze and a very inviting smile. Before I could say anything, he had shot off in his car with a cheerful wave of the hand. John was studying some figures. He pushed the papers down into the pocket of the car when I joined him.

"You found a companion, then," he said.

"M'm. An affable gent."

"A bit flashy. Something to do with films, I believe."

"Is he? I thought he looked as though he belonged to show biz. I wonder what his name is."

"Corinth. Max Corinth. And he's on the production side, I gather."

"And where did you gather that from?"

"Oh, he was in the bar when I went down for a nightcap yesterday evening. He was talking to the American blonde. Her name's Mrs Chagford, but there doesn't seem to be a Mr Chagford around."

"You're in the swim very quickly, John."

"In a bar you can't help picking up these things. People always chat. I wasn't particularly interested. Don't go much for those extrovert types like Corinth myself. A bit of a wolf, I'd say."

"A great big wolf, I'd say. Are you sure you're happy for me to drive?"

"Your car. You drive. And you do it as competently as you do everything else, my dear. I'm quite happy."

"But wishing, perhaps, that you'd got your own Rover here?"

"Not at all. I'd much rather fly. Driving across Europe has no appeal for me. So having your little car and a more than agreeable chauffeuse at my disposal here is an admirable arrangement."

"Bless you, how nice to be with a man who really believes in equality of the sexes!"

"Why not? More comfortable all round."

As I drove back to the hotel, two small pricks registered in my mind, hardly enough to disturb, but there all the same. How could John sit in front of one of the most beautiful views in Europe studying figures? And just what was Mr Max Corinth up to?

John remained abstracted during the drive back to the hotel, and I knew his mind was on business. I could not help thinking of Wordsworth's lines.

> A primrose by a river's brim
> A yellow primrose was to him,
> And it was nothing more.

I stole a glance at him. A good profile. Pleasant features. I had never seen his face register wonder, excitement or emotion. Perhaps that was what had appealed to me in the early days when I had floundered about feeling an emotional wreck. But now I felt that I was looking at a stranger; that underneath the surface, we did not communicate. I shivered, and had the uneasy feeling that some protective casing round me was cracking.

About a mile from the hotel, three climbers emerged from the wooded slopes on to the road ahead of us. Two fair heads and one dark. They were dressed in climbing rig and one of the fair men carried a coiled rope round his shoulder, the other an ice axe.

"Isn't that your friend Ferrion and the two young Austrians from the hotel?" asked John.

"Yes."

"They look tired. Better offer them a lift."

I stopped just ahead of them. They accepted our offer, and somehow crammed into the back of the car. I dropped John and the two Austrians at the hotel entrance, but Gareth came round to the car park with me, wanting to fetch a map from his car. It was then that I discovered that he was the owner of the grey Mercedes which had broken into my peace the previous morning. I made no comment, however, determined to keep everything on a cool, impersonal footing. I lingered by my car, inspecting the loose number plate, hoping Gareth would go on ahead, but he joined me, map in hand.

"Any trouble?"

"The number plate's loose."

He squatted down and inspected it. His thick black hair was an inch from my hand. I drew back, trembling a little, and told myself that I must have caught a cold that afternoon. He looked up at me and gave me an enigmatic little smile.

"Nothing that a screw-driver won't fix. Hold on a sec."

He went across to his car and returned with a screw-driver.

"Enjoyed your day, Kate?" he asked as he worked.

"Very much. And you?"

"Yes, thanks. Climbed the Weisskopf. A good day."

"You're still as keen on climbing, then?"

"Haven't done much for the past few years. Wanted to see if I could still do it."

"Hardly convalescent treatment after that bug."

He squinted up at me.

"That's what I was testing. No excuse for thinking about that bug any more now."

"But you're still going to take a month's leave?"

"Certainly. My first for more than two years. Would you be wanting me to curtail it, Kate?"

"Why should I?"

"Why indeed? You've grazed your leg."

"I know. I did it scrambling down a path this afternoon."

"You should wear more protective clothing on the mountains," he observed, glancing at my short pale blue dress. "But then perhaps you don't expect to rough it. Your companion doesn't appear to be that type, and London seems to have put a smooth coating over you, too."

"As I said, the years have changed me."

"I said a smooth coating. Basically, people don't change all that."

"They grow up."

"They get some armour," he said, grinning. "Are you going to marry that dull fish, Kate?"

"That is my business."

"As an old friend of the family, mayn't I know?"

"Thank you for fixing it," I said coolly as he stood up.

"A pleasure. So you haven't decided to say yes."

"What makes you think that?"

"Because if you had, you'd be only too delighted to tell me."

"How do you know that John even wants to marry me? It is possible for a man and a woman to be friends, you know, without making any more demands of each other. You shouldn't jump to conclusions."

"I don't. But whatever you may think, Castleford's taking it for granted that you're going to marry him."

"And what grounds have you for saying that?" I was getting really angry now.

"Just a remark he let drop in passing. We had quite a cosy chat on our own yesterday morning, after you'd hard-heartedly left us."

"Then why did you ask me?"

"Because I couldn't quite believe that you'd make yourself captive to a dull conventional husband like that, but, of course, he has his points. He'll let you do just what you like, as long as he's not disturbed, and that will suit you, perhaps."

"Precisely," I said acidly.

"Well, I hope you'll invite me to the wedding. I expect to be based in England for some time now. I'd like to be there to wish you a happy future, though I must confess I'm surprised at your choice."

"I don't see why. John would never dominate me so that I lost my own individuality, nor treat me like an old pair of slippers—there whenever wanted."

His dark eyes gleamed with laughter.

"Not old slippers, Kate," he protested. "Never anything resembling old slippers. You'll have to do better with your similes than that when you write."

In vain I clutched at my play-it-cool rôle, knowing that he was deliberately needling me and that by losing my control I was playing right into his hands. Looking at that dark, mocking face, I was shaken by powerful emotions which I was in no state to analyse. I only knew I wanted to hit him. It was years since I had been in a rage like this.

"You're intolerable. My life has nothing to do with you now. Whatever was between us was finished years ago, fortunately for me. And now will you please leave me alone?"

"But it wasn't quite finished, Kate, was it? You left me a letter, remember? When I wanted to talk it over with you, you refused to see me and ran off and went to ground."

"That last row was final enough, surely."

"Nonsense. We both lost our tempers and said more than we really meant. Your letter was about more than that row. I had a right to answer it. You never gave me the chance. Why?"

I wouldn't answer him and tried to brush past him, but he held me firmly by the shoulders.

"Why, Kate? I've a right to know."

"Because you would have beaten down all my arguments and won me over. I never could stand out against you, then. You had all the weapons. Unfair weapons."

"Meaning?"

"Physical ones. You knew that."

"Yes. I wouldn't have used them that time, though."

"You would. You couldn't help it. You were you."

"And the chemistry was powerful," he said with a reminiscent smile. "I'm glad the sophistication is only a veneer and hasn't really gone in deep enough to harden you. And I'm glad you still speak the truth, when cornered."

I couldn't say anything. I felt suddenly exhausted, and leaned back against the car door, perilously close to tears. I had painfully and slowly clawed myself back to peace of mind over the years, had found myself, only to have my smooth, efficient life cracked open again at the first contact with Gareth.

"I know things have changed, Kate," he said quietly. "A lot has happened to both of us in the past four years, and in some ways we *are* different now. I'd still like to have that talk with you some time, though."

"It's irrelevant now."

"Is it? That remains to be proved. Is the chemistry right between you and Castleford?"

"John's a very kind person."

"I'm sure he is, but you haven't answered my question. He'll not make you unhappy, ever. Only bore you to tears. But you'll always have your writing to absorb you, of course."

"Are you always able to predict people's futures so confidently for them?"

"Only Kate's. But then I happen to know her very well. I like the more sophisticated top dressing, by the way. It becomes you. Now I'm more than a bit tired and badly in need of a hot bath. Hope my two mates haven't hogged the only free bathrooms. Coming?"

We walked round to the hotel together. I felt uneasy and baffled. One moment he was playing it as cool as I could have wished, the next he was needling me, then he was serious and kind, only to slide into teasing me again. No wonder I couldn't handle him. And his uncanny penetration was disconcerting, to say the least. After all these years, he came back and walked about in my mind as though those years between had never been.

5

Party Tricks

I WAS WAYLAID by Max Corinth just as I was going into the dining-room that night.

"I'm giving a little birthday party on the terrace after dinner, Kate. It must be Kate," he said with his expansive grin. "Can't be formal on holiday. You and your friend will help me to celebrate, won't you?"

"Well, er, thank you. That's very kind of you. I don't know whether John has work to do, but I'll ask him."

"Do that. If he can't tear himself away from work, all the more reason for you to come. I'm thirty-five today, and although I don't rave about that, it's an excuse for a party. I'll be very disappointed if you don't come. My birthday will be blighted," he declared extravagantly.

"I can't believe that, but I'll be there to wish you many happy returns."

"Fine. Just fine."

John wasn't too pleased at the prospect. He didn't care for the brash Mr Corinth.

"Oh well," he said. "Better put in an appearance, I suppose."

As Corinth had said nothing about it to me at our earlier meeting that day, I assumed that this was a spur-of-the-moment idea, but when we joined the little gathering on the terrace, a long table had been set up with drinks and little dishes of olives and snacks, and an Austrian in folk costume of breeches, short gay jacket, broad leather belt and feathered hat stood in the background, accordion in hand. The party consisted of the proprietor and his wife, Mrs Chagford, Gareth, Mrs Binlay, the two young Austrians, John and myself.

"Give us all a chance to get better acquainted," said Max,

greeting me with enthusiasm and keeping an arm round my shoulders as he shepherded me to a chair. Gareth was talking to Mrs Chagford, and John was led to Mrs Binlay, who smiled up at him charmingly.

There was a good deal of drink going round, and the party soon thawed. I took care to keep away from Gareth, and clung to the protection of either my host or John, according to their availability. And Max Corinth was very available. Come what may, I was not going to be manipulated again out of my cool impersonal rôle with Gareth.

Max was an excellent host, and an entertainment in himself, as was evident when Mrs Chagford asked him about the last film he had worked on, and he gave us a hilarious account of their trials on location in Tunisia. I had never heard a better raconteur, and we were weak with laughter before he had finished. Then he called for some music, and somehow it was Gareth sitting beside me and not Max. I took no notice, sipping my drink, pretending to be absorbed in the music, but every nerve in my body was conscious of his presence.

The lanterns had been lit in the courtyard, making it a place of shadowy enchantment. Quietly, I slipped across to the fountain where John was standing talking to one of the Austrian boys. I put my arm through his as he introduced me to Otto, and he patted my hand as he went on talking about the economics of farming in Austria. Otto was about twenty, I guessed, with the fair good looks of so many of his compatriots. He spoke good English and seemed an intelligent, pleasant young man. Perhaps it was courtesy that made him appear so attentive to John's remarks, for when the accordion player, at Max's request, struck up a Viennese waltz, I fancied I saw a slight expression of relief flit across Otto's face, and when Max cleared some tables from the centre of the courtyard and began to dance with Mrs Binlay, Otto turned to me with a smile and a little bow, and asked if I would care to dance.

"I'm not at all sure that I'll excel at a Viennese waltz," I said, "but I'd love to try."

"It is simple, once you get the rhythm," said Otto, who proved to be so expert that it was simple indeed to follow him, and although the gravelled surface of the courtyard was not ideal to dance on, it was firm enough to make dancing enjoyable. I noticed Mrs Binlay, with an adaptability and charm which her husband's embassy post had doubtless instilled, coping with Max's exuberance with every sign of enjoyment as he swung her round. Mrs Chagford and Gareth did not join in, and indeed I doubted whether the height of her heels and the tight skirt of her elegant blue silk suit would have allowed such freedom of movement. In any case, it seemed to me that Mrs Chagford was not the sort of person to let herself go, even with several drinks inside her. She was talking to Gareth now, smiling up at him. She had lovely slender legs, I thought, as I passed. She did not mix freely with the other guests, and somehow seemed to convey the subtle impression that only Gareth was worthy of serious attention.

"It is good?" said Otto, holding me off a little in the crook of his arm as we circled round.

"Very good. There's a lot to be said for the old fashioned dances."

"They are gay. I like them, too."

After a thirst-quenching interval, Max called for another waltz, and by this time, attracted by the music, some of the hotel staff, encouraged by Max, were joining in.

"Kate, will you crown my evening and dance this with me?" Max asked, looming over me.

"Delighted," I said, for it was impossible not to respond to his lively personality.

I was of average height, but he dwarfed me. Like many big men, however, he was surprisingly light on his feet and no mean performer of a Viennese waltz. I was beginning to enjoy myself very much, caught up in the gay lilt of the music and the charm of the scene in the lantern-lit courtyard. We circled round the centre flower-bed, behind the well-head, past the fountain, weaving in and out to the strains of the Gold and Silver waltz. Max gave me a bear-like hug at the end.

"We'll have another after I've done my duty elsewhere," he said. "You and I go well together, Kate."

He left me, laughing and breathless, beside John, who would have nothing to do with these cavortings.

"It's fun, John," I urged. "Do have just one go. Anybody can waltz."

"I dare say, if they want to. I don't. How long do you think we have to stay? I'm finding it all a bit of a bore."

"We don't *have* to stay at all."

"Oh well, one doesn't want to appear discourteous. Decent of Corinth to invite us. Just not my kind of show. I should think we could thank him and drift off soon, though. That is, unless you really want to stay until the bitter end," he added as an afterthought.

"Yes, I do. I'm enjoying letting my hair down."

"I can see you are. Well, bless you, and why not? You've earned a holiday. Another half hour, then?"

But I could see he was a little surprised at my enthusiasm and that it was an effort for him to indulge me. I jumped at a hand on my shoulder.

"May I have this one with you, Kate?" asked Gareth.

Immediately, I was at panic stations. To be in Gareth's arms, dancing to the insidious lilt of a Viennese waltz in a shadowy courtyard so attuned to romance? Never. On his own, he was menace enough to my peace of mind. With such allies and in my present party mood, I could not answer for myself. With my mind working at the speed of light, I said with scarcely a pause:

"I'm so sorry, Gareth. But I turned my ankle just now and I'm resting it."

"Did you, my dear?" said John, not at his brightest.

"Let's have a look," said Gareth calmly. "Which one?"

"The left," I said quickly.

He knelt down and lifted my left foot in one hand, running the other over the ankle. I wanted to kick him.

"Does that hurt?" he asked, moving it.

"A little."

"Well, the remedy's right by us," he said cheerfully, and before I could guess his intention, he had whipped out a handkerchief from his breast pocket, soaked it in the fountain beside us and slapped it round my ankle, making an icy cold, wet bandage of it. I gasped as the water trickled into my shoe and soaked my stocking.

"Drastic, but effective," said Gareth, standing up and smiling at me. "And now, can I fetch you a drink and something to eat while you look on? I shouldn't use that ankle, if I were you."

Had there been a weapon handy, I really believe I would have used it on him as he stood there in the half light, his dark face mocking me, and for a moment I was choked with anger. It took a great effort to say calmly:

"Thank you. I'd like a lager. Nothing to eat."

"Right."

He weaved his way through the crowd towards the terrace.

"We're going for a walk," I said to John, grabbing his hand. "Quickly."

"My dear girl, what *are* you playing at?" said John as I pulled him through the gateway of the courtyard and started along the track by the stream. "And what about your ankle?" he added as I urged him along. "It's a dark night and the ground's rough."

"There's nothing wrong with my ankle, as Gareth very well knew."

"Then why did you say there was?"

"Oh *John*! I just didn't want to dance with him."

"Well, why not just say you were tired?"

"I spoke on the spur of the moment. I didn't have time to invent a better excuse."

"Well, it seems an odd way to treat an old acquaintance. If you can put up with that chap Corinth, I'd have thought you could have managed a dance with Ferrion, who's a decent enough chap."

Useless to tell John that you needed a long spoon to sup with the devil.

"I have a right to choose who I'll dance with."

"Of course, my dear, but there are ways of handling these social awkwardnesses, and if you'll forgive me for saying so, yours was a bit inept. All you achieved was a wet bandage, and I'm quite sure

Ferrion thought you spoke the truth and was trying to be helpful."

"And how!" I said sceptically.

"Moreover, by using that excuse, you've put yourself out of the running for any more dancing, which wasn't your wish, I'm sure. Really, I'd have thought you could handle things more sensibly than this, Kate."

I rather felt that he was weighing up these unexpected social defects which could handicap me as a hostess if called upon to entertain his business friends. I had made a fool of myself, I knew. Panic had sent my wits flying. The knowledge, however, did not soothe me, and I said rather curtly:

"I don't have to consider Gareth Ferrion's feelings. I shall go back and dance if I wish."

"But that makes you out a liar."

"Gareth knows that. And white lies are permissible, aren't they?"

"Only when they carry at least some conviction," said John.

My sense of humour struggled through, and I said ruefully:

"I admit to fumbling the ball. Put it down to the dancing. My head was in a whirl."

"Well, I don't see what we're achieving by stumbling up this path. We'll both end up with sprained ankles if we're not careful."

"And that would serve me right, but not you," I said, as we stopped by the bridge.

"In any case, my dear, we'll have to go back and thank Corinth for a nice party. We can't just disappear. And even if you don't like Ferrion, and I can't think why, you've surely enough experience at handling people to be able to deal with him in a less childish fashion."

"You'd think so," I said darkly. "Forget it, John. Need we go back? The party must be nearly over now."

"Of course we must. You can't just walk out and not thank your host."

"As you say," I said meekly, and we walked back.

But the party, far from being over, seemed to be building up, for there were more people dancing now than before, and the atmosphere was even more hilarious.

"If you ask me," said John, "there are a few people here who have had more than enough to drink. It's time we said good-night and went."

But Max Corinth was nowhere to be seen. We sat down in the quietest corner we could find to wait until he reappeared. My foot was still cold and wet, although I had pulled off the bandage and thrown it away, and my head was aching slightly. When Otto sought me out for a dance, however, I accepted out of a spirit of devilment. John might think that I had put myself out of the running for dancing by my plea of a strained ankle, but I was not going to give Gareth that victory. I danced, and had the pleasure of whirling past Gareth, who was partnering the fair little hotel waitress, Lise, with his usual expertise.

I could see that John was a little pained by my behaviour, but he made no comment on it when I returned to him.

"Don't know where Corinth has got to," he said. "I shan't wait about much longer. Ah, there he is. Come on, Kate. Let's thank him and get out of this. I've had more than enough."

Max expressed surprise and regret at our premature departure.

"But it's just warming up, folk," he said.

"A splendid evening," said John heartily. "Thanks, my dear chap. Thoroughly enjoyed it. But Kate and I have planned a strenuous day tomorrow, so if you'll excuse us. A splendid birthday party. I congratulate you."

"Well, I'm glad you've enjoyed it. May I rob you of Kate for just one last waltz?"

John looked at me, and I said recklessly:

"Don't wait for me, John. I'll just have this one with Max before calling it a day."

John said good-night and went in.

"Keeps you reined in a bit, Kate, that friend of yours, doesn't he?" observed Max. "Not that I blame him, mind you. But it's good to see you let yourself go and really enjoy yourself. Don't want to take life too seriously."

"I haven't danced for years. And this kind of dancing is infectious."

"I'll say! Come on."

He swept me round, singing to the music of the Merry Widow waltz as he went, and I sang with him, until we finished, breathless, at a table under the mountain ash tree. He was called away then by the waiter, and I was about to go into the hotel, feeling that the evening had been nicely rounded off, when I saw Gareth slipping through the crowd towards me. He blocked my way to the hotel. Just behind me was a little-used gate from the courtyard giving on to a path which led round to the back of the hotel. I was out of my chair and through the gate in the twinkling of an eye, and scampering along the path. I would have gained the hotel safely but luck was against me in the solid form of Franz, staggering along the path with a crate of bottles. I all but ran into him in the dim light.

"It is Miss Danville?" he asked, smiling round the edge of the crate. "This is a thirsty party, *nicht wahr?*"

"It is indeed," I said smiling and edging away, but the slight delay was fatal. Gareth caught me at the corner.

"The ankle's better, I see," he said in a voice I didn't like at all. Smooth and deadly.

"Yes, thank you."

"I'm glad. You can come back to have that drink and give me that dance, after all."

"Oh no."

"Oh yes. You asked for a drink. You shall have it. And I asked for a dance. The excuse you gave is no longer valid. So I'll have it."

"Do you propose to use force, then?" I asked sweetly.

"I don't think that will be necessary."

"Really? You still think you only have to command, and I obey, like a performing animal?"

"You're behaving like a silly, rude child at the moment. What's got into you, Kate? We're at a party. Just because you and I were once engaged and you broke it off, does that mean we can't meet after four years without making rude faces at each other? I'm only asking for common courtesy, after all. For civilised people, that shouldn't be difficult in the circumstances."

It all sounded so reasonable, but underneath, the battle was on, and he knew it. I had been betrayed by panic into behaving like a rude child. In that he was quite right. And at my age, it was absurd. Why did he reduce me to such impotence? There was only one way to fight this, the way I had decided on from the first: coolly, with the confidence which the past years of achievement and experience had brought me. But each time, he had beaten down my cool front leaving me defenceless again except for childish weapons. Once more I tried to muster my defences. I should never get anywhere by defiance. He would never let me get away with that. I spoke quietly.

"I'm sorry, Gareth. I'll come back and have that drink, but do you mind if we skip the dance? I really am tired and the dance I had just now with Max was meant to be the last. I've no more energy left."

He was silent for a moment, then, to my relief, said:

"I'll settle for that. You're frightened of me, Kate, aren't you? I wonder why. You never used to be."

"I told you. I don't want any distractions while I'm here. I came to work."

"I can't see that I'm distracting you from work when we're both at a party."

"I thought perhaps you might get ideas if I relaxed," I said sweetly, back on my mettle now.

"I'm getting ideas all right, but not the ones you have in mind, perhaps. Still opting for a lager?" he asked, opening the gate for me.

"Yes, please."

I sat at a table that had been pushed back into a far corner, glad of the dim light, for I knew my face betrayed me too easily to Gareth's experienced eyes. He had once known me too intimately not to recognise the signals. While he was away fetching the drink, I strengthened my resolution by remembering an incident in the past when at a party I had met an old school friend who had introduced me to her husband. They had been married only a few months. She had invited me to their new house in Chelsea, including my fiancé in the invitation. I had accepted, knowing that we were free that Saturday. Gareth, talking to a friend on the other side of the room, had not looked pleased when I had told him. He disliked the man she had married and nothing would induce him to accept an invitation to his house. And nor must I. "But I've already accepted, Gareth," I'd said. "Then you must go and tell them we can't manage it, after all," he'd replied gently, and his friend had smiled. Gareth's expression had frozen the protest on my lips. He had gone on talking to his friend and I had gone off to my friend and made our excuses, despising myself for it. I remembered it all so vividly. That little smile on his friend's face; Gareth's assumption that I would immediately do as I was told. It was only one of many incidents during the year of our engagement that had left me with a contempt for myself, a contempt only strengthened because in Gareth's arms afterwards any protests were always kissed away and I yielded to him as ardently as ever. Never again, I vowed, as he came back now with two glasses of lager.

"Quite a party," he observed, sitting beside me and watching the dancers. "I fancy we've got some gate-crashers."

"Yes. I've enjoyed it."

"Pace too hot for John? I see he's gone."

"He left me to have a last dance with Max, which I couldn't refuse as he's our host."

"Not quite John's kind of party, perhaps."

"I wouldn't say that. It was nice to get away on our own for a little while, though, even if I did have to be rude to you to do it. You might have been more understanding."

He looked at me quickly but I felt fairly secure in that shadowy light. His voice had an edge to it that told me I had scored, though.

"You should have been more explicit."

"Should I have to spell it out to someone of your years and experience? After all, you know that John and I . . ."

"Are you trying to tell me it was John's idea, then, to fob me off like that?" asked Gareth drily.

"Not exactly. But I knew he was getting restive with all this milling crowd about us."

"He didn't look restive to me. Merely bored. And he's far too well mannered to send anyone off on a phoney errand, or invent lying excuses."

"I know. John's nature is altogether too good for this rough world. That was me, I'm afraid. But I have apologised, and we *did* so want to get away on our own."

"Don't overdo it, Kate. You've made your point."

"I just don't want you to be under any misapprehension."

"I understand. You'll miss John when he goes back at the end of the week."

"Yes. But I shall be able to concentrate on my book by way of compensation."

"How long have you known him?"

"Oh, about three years. He's been a great help to me in many ways."

"I'm sure. I'm glad you made a success of your business as well as your writing, Kate. You needed success to give you confidence."

"Thank you," I said warily.

"Not that I think you trust your new-found confidence as much as you ought. If you did, you wouldn't behave like a frightened rabbit with me."

I was not going to let him drive me into a corner again, and I said coolly:

"That's how you interpret it."

"How else, dear Kate? How else?"

"I should think the obvious interpretation was that I really didn't want to renew our acquaintance. I don't know how I can make it plainer."

"Not a grain of friendship left? After all, even divorced people can be pleasant to each other if they happen to meet again afterwards. You're really a little primitive, Kate, you know."

I choked down my indignation at this case of the pot calling the kettle black. Gareth Ferrion was the least civilised person I knew.

"I told you. No distractions."

"The purposeful business woman and writer, fighting off all friendly contacts for the sake of her work? Come off it, Kate. Your blood doesn't run that cold. You're afraid."

"Of what?" I asked coldly.

"You tell me. All I've done is to ask for the opportunity to answer that letter you wrote me. You seem afraid to give me that opportunity, and it can only be because you're uncertain of your own ground."

"I'm quite certain of it. That's why there's no point in raking up the past. It's quite, quite dead."

"Then why won't you dance with me? Why make such a to-do about a trivial little thing like a dance? If the past's quite dead, it can mean no more to you than dancing with young Otto, or Max Corinth, or anybody else."

"It doesn't. I'm just tired and don't want to dance any more, that's all. Now if you'll excuse me, Gareth, I'll say good-night. Thank you for the drink."

He stood up as I turned to go. A rowdy party had loomed up and one of the men grinned at me and put a hand round my waist. Gareth took my arm, gave the man a look which made him move hastily away, and said:

"I'll see you through this mob. It's getting a bit out of hand."

I was conscious of the pressure of his hand behind my elbow as he shepherded me across. It seemed to set every nerve in my body tingling. Dance with him? Never. And the knowledge that he realised quite well why I would not dance with him did little to comfort me. He released me at the door into the hotel.

"Good-night, Kate. Sleep well. And don't worry," he said with an enigmatic little smile.

And just what did he mean by that, I wondered as I walked upstairs to my room feeling suddenly very weary indeed. Fighting Gareth was hard work. Avoidance still seemed the safest strategy. Perhaps I ought to leave at the end of the week with John. But I had booked for the month and it would be unfair to the Eashers to vacate a room at such short notice. And why should I allow Gareth to drive me out of a hotel I liked and a place I had fallen in love with? Why should he disrupt my plans? I was *not* afraid of him. I would *not* run away. Of course I could cope with the situation.

Reassuring myself vehemently all the while I was getting myself ready for bed, I found it hard to get to sleep when I switched off the light. And my last thought was, keep playing it cool, even if it does infuriate him. He'll get tired of it in time, and give up.

6

Close Quarters

SOMEHOW, THE OLD easy, pleasant relationship between John and me seemed gone when we drove to Innsbruck the next morning. John was detached, his mind obviously on the business matter that had cropped up, and I felt that any effort he made to communicate with me was done out of a sense of duty. Or perhaps it was that I felt edgy. It occurred to me that we got on much better on a workaday footing than on holiday.

John bought some air mail stationery and sent off a cable while I bought some rubber-soled canvas shoes for mountain walking. My sandals did not grip well enough and I intended to go higher in the hills and mountains before I was through.

Over coffee, John apologised for being preoccupied.

"But I know you understand, Kate. That's what I like about you. You have work to occupy your own mind, unlike most women who have to latch on to others all the time."

As long as you don't disturb him, Gareth had said. Confound Gareth.

"Of course I understand, John. This was an awkward time for you to be away, I guess."

"I didn't expect this affair to come to the boil just now. But you mustn't let me clip your wings. I shall have to do an hour's work this afternoon, but you go off on your exploring. You can tell me all about it afterwards. I'm not much of a foot-slogger, anyway."

"All right. If you're sure you won't mind."

"My dear girl, we don't have to shadow each other. As a matter of fact, I've never been a holiday enthusiast myself. I don't mind travelling on business, but that's as far as it goes. If you want any help in keeping Max Corinth at bay, let me know," he added, smiling.

"I can handle him all right."

"I don't doubt it. He greeted you at breakfast this morning as though he was God's gift to you."

"Just his flamboyant manner. He's like that with all females under a certain age, I guess."

"Maybe. Anyway, you can't afford half measures with a skin as thick as that. I think our smart American has her eyes trained on your friend Ferrion, by the way. They were having a very cosy encounter outside one of the bathrooms this morning."

"I wouldn't know," I said, surprised, as I had been before, at this almost old maidish curiosity of John's about other people's affairs.

"Quite a nice set of people in the hotel. Mrs Binlay's a charming woman. Her husband's in the Foreign Office, she tells me."

"I don't think she's quite so charming to her daughter."

"Oh, the girl's at an awkward age. A bit of a trial, I'd say."

I opened the map, feeling suddenly irritated, and began to study it for likely walks. John lit a cigarette and looked around him. We were bored with each other, I thought. Too much time together. We could only be happy together in small doses, it seemed.

That afternoon I decided to do some serious work on the plot of my new book, and to that end, found a quiet spot under a birch tree on the hill behind the hotel, and firmly dismissed both Gareth and John from my head. After a sticky start, during which my ball point pen ran dry and I had to make a quick trip to the hotel to get another, I really got into it, and before I knew where the time had gone it was after six and I had missed my tea. That being so, I worked on for another half hour before returning to the hotel in time to bath and change for dinner. I found on my bed a guide book to the district. I supposed Max Corinth had given it to the porter for me when he found I was out, although why he couldn't have waited until he saw me, I didn't know. I thanked him when I met him on the stairs on my way down to dinner. His response was an expansive smile and a friendly hand on my shoulder.

John seemed constrained at dinner.

"Anything wrong?" I asked, as we went out to the courtyard to have our coffee there, for the evening was beautifully warm again.

"Well, you know I'm broad-minded, Kate, but aren't you making a bit of a fool of yourself over that chap Corinth?"

I stared at him in amazement.

"What on earth makes you say that? I've hardly spoken two sentences to him today."

"No?"

"No. What's on your mind?"

"I happened to be chatting to Ferrion in the corridor upstairs just after I'd had tea, and we saw Corinth come out of your room. At least, I knew it was your room. Perhaps Ferrion didn't."

"So what? He'd left a guide book on the bed for me. I found it there when I got back this evening."

"As he came out of the room, he said, 'Thanks a lot, honey'."

"Then it must have been a chamber-maid he was talking to. I was out all the afternoon."

"I saw you come back to the hotel soon after three."

"To fetch another Biro. The one I had with me had gone dry. The guide book wasn't there then."

"There are no chamber-maids about in the afternoon."

"So you think I'm lying?"

"My dear girl, there's no need to get so intense. I would merely suggest that you show more discretion. You don't want people drawing wrong conclusions."

"I can't help it if Corinth chose to leave a book in my bedroom while I was out, and I don't see anything exactly immoral in that."

"Well, let's say no more about it," said John impatiently. "But that chap's a wolf. You said it yourself. You should steer clear of him if you don't want to get tarred with his brush."

"Let's get this straight, John. Either you think I'm lying and that Max Corinth and I were getting together in my room this afternoon, which is so ludicrous that I could laugh if I weren't so annoyed, or else you believe me and accept that there must have been a chamber-maid in that room this afternoon when Corinth left the book."

"My dear, you're dramatising all this," said John calmly. "Not like you. Forget it. I just don't want people to draw wrong conclusions about you, as Ferrion might, and start up some gossip. Hence the warning. For heaven's sake don't let's make a storm in a tea-cup. You haven't seemed your usual well-balanced self since we've been here. Do you feel all right?"

"Never better," I snapped, and accepted a refill of my coffee cup from Franz.

John began to talk quite affably about the Test Match now in progress at home, a subject which did not interest me in the slightest. He had backed down on the subject of Corinth because he really didn't want to be disturbed, but if he had any feeling for me, he should have been disturbed. He obviously did not believe that I wasn't in that room with Corinth but was not prepared to go further. What sort of a cold man was he not to be angry with me if he thought that? And how little he knew me if he could think that I would fall so readily for a man like Max Corinth and lie about it. All he seemed to care about was what other people would think. Dismayed, I sat there listening to him talking about cricket, realising that I had thought I knew John Castleford well enough to contemplate marrying him and sharing his life, when in fact I had known nothing about him. What sort of judgment was that? Where was my boasted ability about being able to run my own life so satisfactorily? I tried to comfort myself with the fact that I hadn't really decided, but the knowledge that I had come so near appalled me.

That night, in bed, I went back over the recent years, trying to see how I could have been so blind, and I realised that John's very absence of feeling, of demands on me, had been welcome after the storms which had shaken the very roots of me. My mistake had been to think that there could ever have been more than a surface-skimming friendship between us. I was grateful to him for that. I had needed it. And he had thought my blood was of the same cool category because I had thrown myself into my work at a time when I was emotionally exhausted and needed that impersonal landscape for recovery. Neither of us was to blame. Being thrown together on holiday had merely revealed the underlying differences between us. I fancied that the revelation was just as discomfiting to John as to me. I wasn't the young woman he had taken me for. Fortunately, neither of us would be deeply hurt. A faint disappointment for John, perhaps, but no more; for me a feeling of uncertainty in my own judgment and a little soreness at John's lack of trust in me over this foolish Corinth affair.

We were both especially nice to each other for the remainder of that week. I went off on my own when John said he had work to do, for which he always apologised most sincerely. Otherwise, we drove about the country, spent a lot of time drinking coffee in cafés or in the hotel courtyard, invariably courteous and considerate to each other, perhaps because we both felt a little guilty about each other and embarrassed at that show of naked feeling over Corinth.

I was able to get no satisfaction out of that gentleman when I asked him if there had been anybody else in my room when he left the book, for he gave me a bland negative, and when I told him that John had had the impression that he was talking to somebody there, he merely shrugged his shoulders with a charming grin and said John must have been mistaken.

I avoided Gareth as far as possible that week. I had decided to follow my father's advice and steer clear of men. I was back on the bachelor-girl stance. And Gareth could draw whatever conclusions he liked about Corinth's visit to my bedroom. Not that he was likely to be interested, for Mrs Chagford was, as John had said, making a set at Gareth whenever he was available, which was not often for he spent most of the days out climbing with the two Austrians. When we did meet, we were not alone, and I was beautifully polite.

On John's last evening, we went into the village after dinner to have drinks in the beer garden behind the inn, where there was singing and folk dancing. I noticed Gareth and Mrs Chagford there, too, but there were several tables between us and them and I pretended not to see them. I did not enjoy the entertainment as much as I might otherwise have done because I was wondering how to tell John that my answer was still no without hurting his pride.

On the walk back to the hotel, he took my arm and said: "You're quiet this evening. What's bothering you?"

In the end, I thought, there was no way but the direct.

"John, I know I said I'd give you my answer to your proposal at the end of my stay here, but my mind is made up now. I'm truly grateful for your friendship, but I want it to stay like that."

He said nothing for a few moments, then squeezed my arm.

"All right, Kate. I'll accept that as final. And we'll still be good friends, as we have been before?"

"Yes, please. I'm sorry if I've disappointed you."

"Nothing to reproach yourself with. You've never misled me and have always maintained that you liked your single state. You're probably right. I'm a bit set in my ways, too. We'll forget it and just put the clock back."

I was relieved that he was not distressed by my decision; indeed, a mocking little demon inside me suggested that he might be a little relieved, since I was not quite the calm, easy proposition he had thought me, and marriage involved some upheaval, however coolly approached. And perhaps it was a mutual relief that put us suddenly in very good spirits, and when John left me in the courtyard to go and do his packing, for he was leaving early the next morning, he put his arms round me and gave me a very affectionate kiss.

"Good-night, Kate. I'm as fond of you as ever, remember."

"Bless you," I said, kissing his cheek.

I heard a woman laugh nearby as John went off, and I turned quickly and went out of the courtyard and round the hotel to the track up the hill, for it was a fine night and I felt suddenly energetic, released by the reassurance of having cleared up the situation with John, and no damage done. Gareth must have followed me, for I heard footsteps behind me before I reached the first bend, and some instinct told me they were his. I did not look back, but he called me as I reached the bend. I walked round it as though I hadn't heard, then instead of following the track, doubled back like a hare, scrambling over a grassy bank into the pine wood through which I could regain the rear of the hotel. The moon penetrated the trees only in odd shafts, but it was enough to make progress possible. I stopped once in dark shadow to look back and listen, but there was no sound but the faint stir of branches in the gentle breeze. In more leisurely fashion, with the lights of the hotel twinkling through the trees now and again to keep me in the right direction, I emerged from the wood only a few yards from the steep bank which sloped down to the car park. My shoes were not very good for the job, and I took the slope at a cautious slither. I landed straight into the arms of Gareth at the bottom.

"Good evening, Kate," he said in a grim voice which warned me of trouble.

Summoning up my determination to keep playing it cool, I spoke as though it was the most natural thing in the world to emerge from a wood at this late hour and scramble down a bank in a cream sheath of a dress, a filmy stole round my shoulders and light kid sandals on my feet.

"Good evening. Trouble with the car?" The Mercedes was only a few yards off.

"What makes you think that?" he asked in a smoothly menacing voice which set my skin prickling.

"I couldn't think of any other reason for your being here at this time."

"But you're here."

"Oh," I said with a laugh and a shrug. "I was just taking a short cut back to the hotel after deciding that I'd had enough walking for today. Good-night."

He caught my arm in a not too kindly grip.

"One can have enough walking, I agree. It's a nice night for a drive, though. Get in."

He had the car door open. I registered polite surprise at the idea, thinking even now that I could handle it coolly.

"Thank you, but no. I'm for bed."

"Get in, Kate, or be thrown in."

"You're being somewhat melodramatic, Gareth, aren't you? Do you mind letting go of my arm? I don't go for this kind of act."

He smothered a word which I guessed was not polite and before I could move a step, had picked me up and half thrown, half bundled me into the car. I was unfamiliar with the door handle, and was only half out by the time he was in the driving seat grabbing me back. He leaned across and slammed my door shut again, and a second later the Mercedes moved off smoothly without a murmur and we were sweeping down the track from the hotel before I could get my breath.

"This is ridiculous!" I exclaimed.

"Shut up," said Gareth.

I sat there, boiling, as he turned left at the end of the drive and drove out of the valley and up the mountain road. Had I been in a different frame of mind, I should have delighted in the beauty of the mountains in the moonlight, the silvery peaks contrasting with the black pinewoods below, the smooth power of the car as it climbed effortlessly; but I was far too angry to be receptive. And beneath the anger was a chill little feeling of fear. He stopped the car almost at the top of the pass, drawing off the road at a parking bay which gave a magnificent panorama of the mountains. The silence was deathly when he switched off the engine, and I thought he must hear my heart beating. I turned to him furiously.

"What sort of stunt is this? How dare you behave like some he-man in a cheap thriller?"

"That's better. Unfortunately, I have to make you angry before you'll stop play-acting with me. I wanted a little chat with you."

"But I don't want any little chat with you."

"You don't have to tell me. That smart bit of work after you heard me tonight made it quite clear that you didn't want to chat, my dear. Why?"

I searched for the most off-putting words my mind would conjure up, and by an enormous effort I made my voice steady and cold.

"You bore me," I said, "like a stale old gramophone record."

He gave a short laugh.

"You've registered many things at our encounters, but boredom was not one of them. I like to see your face when you're lying. Say it again, Kate."

He had switched on the light and turned my face to his with a hard hand under my chin. There seemed to be dark brooding depths in his concentration on me that made me shiver. The grim mouth, the smouldering anger in the dark eyes which swept over me and then came back to mine, warned me that he was in a dangerous mood. For the life of me I couldn't answer him, and he released me with a chilling little smile.

"You're a bad liar. Shall we dispense with lies and play-acting? I want to get things straight. Are you going to marry John Castleford?"

"What business is it of yours?"

"I couldn't think what you saw in him, but now I'm beginning to see a possible reason why he might appeal as a husband. He'd be complaisant enough, I dare say, as long as you were discreet. Is that what you want, Kate? Someone who'll turn a blind eye if you feel like amusing yourself elsewhere?"

"Meaning?"

"Max Corinth, for one."

"You believe that of me?"

"I'm asking you. I wouldn't even have asked the old Kate I knew, but London's permissiveness, or perhaps you see it as freedom, has had its influence on you, perhaps."

"Perhaps."

"Don't push me too far, Kate. The truth now, in this car, tonight, even if we never address one more word to each other afterwards. Corinth. What's going on there?"

I was going to stall again, but something in his expression stopped me in my tracks. He looked capable of violence. I sighed and spoke with what I hoped was withering contempt.

"Max Corinth kindly left a guide book in my bedroom while I was out. He had promised it to me. You and John happened to see him coming out. I can't help it if people have grubby minds."

"He was talking to somebody in there."

"John had the same impression, but when I asked Corinth, he said John was mistaken."

"Oh no he wasn't. My hearing is very good."

"Then it must have been a chamber-maid there. Does it matter? He just left a book for me."

"It took him about an hour."

I turned to Gareth, startled.

"*What?*"

"I happened to see him knocking at your door when I came up to write some letters. I'd finished and was going down to post them when I met Castleford and we both saw Corinth emerge from your room. I'd been writing in my room for the best part of an hour."

"Then he must have had an arrangement with somebody to use my room while I was out. Oh no, it's preposterous. Are you sure?"

"Well, he could have knocked and gone away, and come back again when a chamber-maid was there and left the book. It sounds a bit potty, though, doesn't it?"

"Yes."

"Particularly as he was there again this afternoon."

"Oh no! For how long?"

"I don't know. I saw him coming out about three o'clock. He didn't see me. You weren't there?"

"No. I was up the hill, working. Mrs Binlay's daughter was with me, if you'd like proof."

"Your word is enough. You evidently don't lock your door. May I suggest that in future you do?"

"But I've no valuable jewellery. No money there. Only travellers' cheques. You're not suggesting..."

"I'm not suggesting anything. But Max Corinth has been in your room twice in your absence. So lock your door in future."

"I will. But I can't believe that he's after anything I've got."

Gareth shrugged his shoulders.

"Perhaps just a convenient room for a spot of fun. He's on very friendly terms with that fair chamber-maid."

"But why my room?"

"You may be the only one not to lock it."

"Do you lock yours?"

"Always."

"But why not his own room for fun and games?"

"It's next door to the linen and store room. Mrs Easher's often in and out there. Could be awkward. Your room is tucked away at the far end of the corridor."

"And you thought I'd be willing to amuse that playboy?"

"I thought it unlikely. Extremely unlikely. But I wanted it cleared up. And I thought a word of warning wouldn't come amiss. I don't know what friend Max is up to, but he's not the sort to get mixed up with unless you like getting your fingers burnt."

"You still don't realise that I'm a grown-up person, capable of looking after myself, do you?"

"I'd say you're better at it than you used to be. I'm not so sure about your judgment, though. Castleford? Not really your type, Kate. Nothing in common. Not even the chemistry. That was a very affectionate embrace this evening, but more fatherly than loverly. Have you settled for that for the rest of your life?" He turned my face to his again as I remained silent. "Have you, Kate?"

I would dearly have liked to say yes. I knew it would stop his attacks on me. If I were engaged, he would see it as a contract and not try to undermine it. I fell back on the old formula.

"I still maintain that it's none of your business, Gareth, and I shan't tell you."

He let me go with an odd little smile.

"I'm glad you didn't settle for him. I might have been a bad husband, but he'd have driven you crazy with boredom. Keep him for the accounts."

"John is a much kinder man than you have ever been, or could be," I hurled at him.

"It's easy to be kind when you don't much care. It becomes almost a habit. And what a strain, always having to be kind in return!"

I looked at his dark, sardonic face and felt the old helplessness seize me. With all the new armour I had acquired over the years, I still couldn't get the better of him. He was too clever for me. I tried again.

"I really don't know why you think I'm still interested in what you think, Gareth. The past is quite dead. For me it was buried years ago. I don't know why I have to keep on telling you. I wouldn't go back to the kind of domination you had over me for all the tea in China. I've made a very satisfactory life for myself. The past is irrelevant to it. As dead as mutton."

"Is it? Your words say one thing, your every action another. Let's put it to the test, shall we?"

Before I knew what was happening, he was sitting in my seat with me in his arms. I struggled, but in the end he had me firmly pinned down, my legs sprawled across the driving seat.

"Dead, is it, Kate?" he said, his eyes searching my face.

Then his head blotted out the roof of the car and I closed my eyes as his mouth claimed mine. It seemed as though there was a cloak of thick black velvet against my eyes, and my heart was racing. I stood out against him as long as I could. When I stopped resisting, his lips became more gentle and his hand moved softly in my hair, and I felt the old magic working and lost the fight against the clamour of senses long deprived. When he released me I was trembling and dizzy, with no breath for words, but a bitter protest in my mind.

"I think that disposes of that myth, Kate," said Gareth quietly after a few minutes of silence.

"It was always your weapon. You think that answers everything. That I can be manipulated by it. Subdued, as I was before. It's abominable of you to use it against me now."

"Unfair, yes. But I had to know. And I had to break down this artificial barrier you've thrown up in a sort of panic. But I agree that it doesn't answer everything. Will you make a bargain with me?"

He slid back to the driving seat and I put an unsteady hand to my ruffled hair. His mood had changed. He was serious now, but I felt like an ineffectual bather washed up by a rough sea, floundering in the surf of the waves that had battered me, as he went on:

"I'll give you my word not to use that weapon again if you'll promise not to play-act with me any more."

"Very well," I gulped. "I promise." I couldn't very well go on playing it cool after what had just happened, anyway. He had cracked that defence once and for all.

"We're on holiday here for three more weeks. You want to work on your book. I shall be climbing most of the time, I expect. But if and when we're together, be yourself. Damn it, we've known each other for years, and when our engagement was broken, it didn't make us enemies. You've been running from me as though I was the devil."

"I didn't want to get enmeshed again."

"For the same reasons that you gave in that letter?"

"Yes."

"But we're older now, and I'd like to take you up on that letter in the light of what we've both, perhaps, learned. You never gave me a chance to answer it."

"I like my freedom, Gareth. You will always dominate. It's your nature. I see no point in talking about it any further."

"Right," he said, and his voice was hard again. "I won't raise it any more. When you're ready to talk, let me know. *You* shall ask for that unfinished business to be completed, not I. There comes a time to stop asking."

"You're sure I'll want to? How vain men are!"

"Not vain, Kate. I just know that you belong to me. Don't you?"

"*No.*"

He laughed and in the topsy-turvy sea of emotions which this encounter had evoked, I was back now on the crest of a wave of anger.

"Not to worry," he said cheerfully. "We've made our bargain."

"Why not be satisfied with the flattering attentions of Mrs Chagford?" I asked caustically.

"She's certainly a very agreeable companion for the evenings."

"A pleasant diversion after you've spent the day on man's work."

"Precisely. Anyway, it would be ungallant to refuse her invitations to join her sometimes."

"I've noticed how hard you struggle to avoid them."

"You're a much better fighter than you used to be, Kate. You were all gentle and dewy-eyed once. And so yielding."

"A far preferable proposition for you."

"Not at all. I like the new Kate. Most stimulating."

"A challenge to your ego?"

"Oh boy, what a challenge!" he said with such gusto that I had to laugh in spite of my anger.

"You'll get your come-uppance one day, and I hope I'm there to see it," I said.

"I hope you are, too. Then you can put a loving poultice on my wounded pride."

"Are we going to sit here all night talking nonsense?"

"No. From the bend of the road up there, there's a simply superb view of the Wildspitze in the distance. Let's walk up there and have a look at it before we go back. You've done enough sitting about in cars looking at views through a windscreen with Castleford, I bet. He may be one of those men who prefer to substitute four wheels for two feet, but that's no reason for you to get lazy. I can show you the mountain I'm tackling tomorrow, too."

"Right," I said.

He got out without removing the car keys, I noticed. You shall pay for that crack at John, my lad, I thought, and pretended to be fumbling with my sandal when he opened my door.

"Be with you in a sec. I'm in a state of disarray. A bear hugged me," I said.

He grinned and strolled on up the road. He had swung the Mercedes round to face the way home when he had parked it. I waited until he had almost reached the bend, then slid into the driving seat, turned the ignition key and started the engine. I saw

Gareth turn instantly and begin to run back, but the Mercedes responded like a thoroughbred and slid smoothly round the first bend. I concentrated on my driving but found the big car surprisingly easy to handle. It was only a few minutes' drive back to the hotel, and I parked the car in its usual place.

I went to find Franz before going to bed.

"Mr Ferrion asked me to let you know that he'll be late in tonight, so would you not lock up? He's doing a moonlight walk."

"In preparation for his climb tomorrow? What energy!"

"He certainly is a very energetic man," I glanced at my watch. Nearly eleven. Remembering it was down hill all the way, I reckoned Gareth would need an hour and a half, walking briskly. "He said he'd be back about twelve-thirty."

"I'll leave the door. And perhaps a bottle of lager or a flask of coffee left out would be welcome."

"More than welcome, I'm sure. Good-night, Franz."

"Good-night, Miss Danville. We're promised another fine day tomorrow."

I walked up the stairs to my room in a very happy mood. I might buy myself a Mercedes one day, I thought. It would be worth saving up for.

7

Ann

GARETH AND THE two Austrians had left before John and I had breakfast the next morning. The car John had hired to drive him to Innsbruck was late and he went off a little annoyed at this lapse, although in fact he had allowed plenty of time. John, a punctual person himself, expected punctuality in others. He had refused my offer to drive him to Innsbruck, saying he wouldn't dream of my sacrificing the best part of a morning but I suspected that he really preferred the spaciousness of a hired car and the opportunity to do some work in it. His brief-case was at the ready by his side as he waved good-bye.

I met Ann Binlay as I left the hotel. She was hovering round the fountain in the courtyard, and her face lit up when she saw me.

"Hullo. What's your programme this morning?" I asked.

"I haven't got one. Mother and Roger have gone to the village. I thought I'd just wander along the stream again and photograph some flowers."

I had wanted to do some work on the plot of my book, but the look in her eyes reminded me of a hopeful dog looking at its lead.

"I'm going that way. Shall we go together?"

"If you're sure I won't be in the way. I expect you want to concentrate on your work."

I had had to explain the nature of the notes I was taking at our last encounter along the stream, and she had taken such elaborate precautions not to disturb me then that I had felt guilty.

"Oh, I'm only making rough notes," I said as we set out.

In fact, she did not intrude at all, but wandered around on her own as soon as I had settled myself against a rock. She had a little camera with which she was taking colour photographs of all the wild flowers she found.

"A record for my father. He's interested in botany," she explained.

It was not Ann who was getting between me and the creation of fictitious characters, but the dark, mocking face of Gareth Ferrion. Perhaps I'd better stick to descriptive notes of my surroundings and leave plotting until my mind was better able to concentrate. Somehow, my expectation of a peaceful holiday which would offer me the first opportunity I had had of concentrating entirely on my writing was not being fulfilled. My mind was more confused and preoccupied now than for years past. It was as though I had been encased in my little business world, with three parts of me sleeping peacefully; the troublesome parts that I thought I had tamed and organised. Now they had been dragged out of my casing, tossed up in the air and shaken about as though a terrier had got hold of them, and there was no doubt about the name of that terrier.

The sun was hot, and there was a buzz of insects around me. The water splashed along, its eddies and swirls and smooth patches endlessly fascinating to the eye. I wondered where Gareth and the Austrians had got to. Were they chipping their way up a glacier, cutting steps in a snowfield, or were they still below the snow line? He had always been a keen climber, with a particular liking for his native Welsh mountains. Or should one say half-native? Gareth's mother was Welsh, his father, English. He was not going to get the better of me. I had fought that battle once, without half the equipment that I had now. But I could still wince at the recollection of the pain of it, and the misery of those months afterwards.

I pulled my mind back to the present. Ann was lying full length on her stomach, an insignificant pink flower in the grass the apparent object of her attention. She flattened the grass in front of it, placed a coin beside it for scale, and squinted through the viewfinder of her camera. Intent, her straw-coloured hair spiky against her reddened neck, her cotton frock wrinkled far up her thighs, her long legs splayed out across the grass, she looked so young and vulnerable that I felt a rush of warm affection swamp me, a protective urge which made me want to take her under my wing; a vain wish because I knew only too well that in the end, we all have to fight our own battles. I walked over to her as she sat up, her picture taken.

"What is it?" I asked, squatting beside her.

"I can't find it in my book. I think it's a kind of saxifrage. I found some wild pansies over there."

"Show me."

We pottered around happily, poking under boulders and ferns, until it was nearly lunch time.

"If you've nothing planned for this afternoon, would you like to come for a drive in the mountains with me and see a glacier at close quarters? I was so fascinated by it the other day that I thought I'd pay it a return visit."

Her eyes shone.

"I'd love to. Thank you very much. It's most awfully kind of you."

"I'll be glad of your company. Your neck looks sore. Oughtn't you to put some protective cream on it?"

"Yes. I'll get some in the village next time I'm there. My skin's awful. It always goes red and burns, never goes a nice brown."

"Foolish to try to tan, then. We can stop in the village on our way out this afternoon. We'll leave about two, shall we?"

Her face expressed such grateful pleasure at this prospect that I felt almost ashamed, and angry. What sort of parents had she to make her so pathetically grateful for such crumbs of attention?

The afternoon was a great success, Ann's whole-hearted enthusiasm feeding my own. We had a late tea at a chalet half-way up a mountain, and Ann demolished the most enormous slice of Sachertorte I had yet come across, a chocolate and cream concoction that seemed a little too rich for me that day, although I had sampled a more modest sample of these delicious cakes at a café in Innsbruck. Awkwardly, Ann tried to pay the bill.

"On you next time," I said.

"This has been a lovely day," said Ann, wiping her chocolate marked fingers on her handkerchief. "The best I can ever remember."

"We must have some more," I said, relinquishing all idea of any long spells of work for the next two weeks.

"That would be super. Are you sure I'm not interrupting your work, though?"

"Oh, I'm taking in reams of impressions just as you're taking photographs. They'll all be there for me to use when the time comes. Are you really going to be able to eat any dinner tonight?"

"I expect so," she said cheerfully. "You know, I can't see why you should bother with me. It's so kind of you."

"Not at all," I said crisply. "You should put a higher value on yourself. Other people are apt to take you at your own valuation, you know."

She thought about this, then said:

"But I don't rate much to myself. I know I'm a hopeless mess. Other girls of my age are so . . . different. Confident, capable, even the plain ones like me."

"Inside, we're probably none of us as confident as we've learned to look. Don't keep comparing yourself with other girls. You're an individual. Respect your own individuality. That is always my father's advice, and he, I have always thought, is a very wise man. We shall be late for dinner if we don't move, though you're going to find it difficult with all that Sachertorte inside you."

She grinned and we went back to the car. This time there were no weary climbers to be picked up on the way, and I wondered whether Gareth was back and what sort of reception I should get after last night's escapade.

In fact, he took it very well. The three of them came in late to dinner, but Gareth joined me afterwards at my table by the fountain in the courtyard, carrying his cup of coffee.

"A good day?" I asked warily.

"Splendid. That's why I'm in too lenient a mood to beat you for last night. If you'd smashed the car up I'd have wrung your neck, though."

"I can drive," I said meekly.

"So I gather. The cool nerve of it!"

"You bought it."

He eyed me reflectively and I felt my colour rising.

"Perhaps," he said with a wry grin. "Anyway, don't think you'll get away with it. It's chalked up. I shall take my revenge at a suitable moment. As a matter of fact, I quite enjoyed the walk back, once I'd curbed the strong language. Don't do it again, though. What have you been up to today in the absence of your business adviser?"

I told him.

"What about all this work from which you would brook no distractions?" he said.

"Distraction seems to have broken in, unfortunately. And that child's lonely."

"Terribly hard not to be involved, isn't it? Here you were, all nicely buttoned up. The cool, efficient, detached Miss Danville, complete with business adviser, all set for a spot of useful work. And now other people are breaking in and spoiling the whole organisation."

"You read me like a book. Mrs Chagford's looking hungrily in your direction. Oughtn't you to take pity on her?"

"And leave you in solitude?"

"I can bear it."

"Your friend Corinth is just bearing down on her. I can continue to take pity on you," he said, trailing his coat for me.

"You're so much kinder than you used to be, Mr Ferrion."

"Age mellows us all, we hope. Has your lame duck left school?"

I told him about her, since this seemed a harmless topic, and was a little surprised at his sympathy. Lame ducks weren't his cup of tea, I'd always thought.

"What about her brother? He seems a lively kid. Wants me to take him climbing, if you please. No lack of confidence there."

"He's Ann's half-brother. And from a boy of fifteen, she says, you can't expect much."

"H'm. A bit hard on kids, second marriages. Mrs Binlay evidently dotes on Roger. The good lady doesn't seem to have much sense of fair play. A tough handicap for a girl not well endowed. You'd better try to get some of your spunk into her, Kate."

"She's not weak. Just lacks confidence. And badly needs affection."

"Don't we all?"

"Some more than others. Max Corinth doesn't seem to have your charm. Mrs Chagford's gone in. She doesn't look very pleased."

"She's expecting a telephone call from a friend who's looking in here on his way to somewhere else. I think the gentleman's proving a bit dilatory."

"Mr Chagford?"

"No. She's divorced. This is just a friend, I gather."

"She looks very ... successful."

"M'm. And as hard and ruthless as any business tycoon. She's interesting, though. Travelled a lot. Certainly knows her way around, does Mrs Shirley Chagford."

"She seems a bit out of her element here. I can't help thinking she'd be more at home in a Hilton hotel."

"Yes. She thinks this is a little primitive. And talking of successful women, tell me about your business, Kate. Castleford made you sound like a tycoon, too."

"It just came about. I hired myself out as a temporary typist wherever I was needed, and found I'd more work offered me than I could accept. So I spread from my one room to a small office and took on an assistant, and it mushroomed. I never meant to build up a business. Only wanted to earn enough to keep me while I tried to get a book published."

"How big a business is it now?"

"Oh, quite small, really. We're ten in all. Six permanent typists, a filing clerk cum office girl, a book-keeper, my assistant and I. We do all kinds of typing, but writers form our biggest group of clients. And all my girls are willing to travel and do work on the spot if necessary."

"I'll know where to come then, if I'm stuck for a typist. Do you mean to go on expanding?"

"No. I'm thinking of handing over most of the management to my assistant so that I can concentrate on writing. Once I feel confident of being able to earn enough as a writer, I shall quit altogether, find a cottage in the country and really get down to it," I said firmly, making it clear that I had everything mapped out.

"Sounds a good plan."

"Did you enjoy the job in Africa?"

"Yes. It was interesting. Not an easy project, though, and labour was tricky, so I wasn't altogether sorry when it was finished. The climate rather got me once that bug had bitten."

"Any more foreign jobs in view?"

"No farther than Scotland at present."

"Are you going to live in London permanently?"

"My plans are vague. I've only been back a few weeks."

I looked at him thoughtfully, then said:

"What *did* make you come here, Gareth? It's too big a coincidence to swallow."

"When we have that talk, I'll tell you," he said blandly, and then stood up as Mrs Binlay came to our table to thank me for taking Ann for the drive that afternoon.

"So kind of you," she said with a smile. "My husband has taken our car back to England, so we aren't getting around very much here."

She accepted Gareth's offer to order drinks, and sat down beside me while he went off to fetch them. She was a pretty woman, mid-fortyish, with auburn hair, grey eyes, and an appealing manner. Petite, well dressed, I could imagine that she would be very good at the social duties imposed by her husband's position. She talked to us about France and their life there, and didn't mention the children until I asked her about Ann's future. Then she sighed with a deprecating little shrug of her shoulders.

"We're going to try a secretarial training for lack of any better idea, but her father and I have found it difficult to decide what would be best for her. Unfortunately, she hasn't inherited his brains or his looks. She takes after her mother. A nice girl, but a wee bit of a problem. Fortunately, Roger presents no difficulties. He wants to be a civil engineer, like you, Mr Ferrion. I've heard so much about the African dam project you've been supervising that I feel I've been out there myself. And he's so thrilled with your book. I shall have to watch him to make sure he gives it back."

"He could keep it, except that it's a copy I promised a friend. In fact, I brought it with me to give to my friend before I left him at Heidelberg on my way here, and then forgot it. But there's no hurry. I can post it back any time."

"It's most kind of you to let him borrow it. Copies must be precious to you. I shall make a point of buying it for him as soon as we get back to England. Knowing the author, it's a must. Who is your friend in Heidelberg? We've spent several holidays there and know quite a few people."

"His name's Ian Renton, but I doubt whether you'd know him. He has a research job in that area."

"Ian Renton? No, I don't recognise the name."

"Not surprising, since he's a very anti-social Scot. What sort of training have you in mind for Roger?"

"Oh, a university course for a degree in civil engineering, and then practical training. That's why I'm so glad that this upheaval in our lives is taking place now so that Roger can go to an English university. That's the best course to take, don't you agree?"

"I do. It's a long grind, but worth it."

"A man's career," said Mrs Binlay with an admiring smile for Gareth. The art of flattery was one which she practised with great skill. "Taming nature, you might say."

"Doing our best," said Gareth.

When she left us, I turned to Gareth.

"Come clean. What book?"

"On the great engineering feats of the eighteenth and nineteenth centuries. Harbours, canals, bridges, railways. A great age for engineers."

"You wrote it?"

"Yes."

"When?"

"The year after my girl broke with me. I needed something to distract my mind. It was published a year before yours."

"Stealing my one little piece of thunder. I might have known!"

He grinned, saying:

"Have no fear. I'm no rival. My one and only effort. I've no vocation for writing. Always been interested in that period of engineering, that's all. I was talking about it one day to a publisher pal of Ian's, and he more or less commissioned me to do it. Corrie and Birch, for your information."

"Good publishers. May I see it when Roger's done with it?"

"Of course."

"I hadn't heard about it, Gareth."

"Why should you? Not exactly an earth-shattering event."

"But you'd heard about mine and congratulated me."

"I saw an advertisement. You've a vocation for creative writing. I haven't. Mine was merely a collating of material with a few assessments of my own plus stunning photographs. Anyone interested could have done it. As a matter of fact, I haven't given it a thought since I was away. When Ian knew I was going to pay him a visit, he asked me to bring a copy. Then I forgot to leave it with him and brought it on here. It was no more than an exercise to distract my mind. It's just about paid its way and bought one seat of the Mercedes, I'd say. No reason at all to make a song about it."

But I felt guilty all the same, and saw myself as a monster of indifference until I met his quizzical gaze and realised how crazily irrational I must seem.

"I'm for bed," I said briskly.

"No moonlight drive?"

"It mightn't be so easy this time."

"You bet it wouldn't."
"Good-night, Gareth."
"Good-night, dear Kate."

I went to bed, feeling all at sea again. As well try to handle slippery soap as keep Gareth Ferrion in his place.

8

Sleight-of-Hand

I SPENT MOST of the second week of my holiday with Ann, and enjoyed it, thrusting all personal problems from my mind. Gareth was out climbing most days. Sometimes he joined me in the evenings and we talked about the day's exploits. I kept the conversation to impersonal topics as firmly as I could, and apart from one or two sly digs he followed suit. I knew he would keep his promise, and to that extent I felt less threatened. I ought to have felt completely carefree, since he had laid down that it was I who should make any further approach to that old footing, but in fact I was feeling less sure of myself than I wished to be. Only a little more than two weeks, and the holiday would be over and we shall be going our separate ways again, I reminded myself. But even now that Gareth had tied his own hands, I still felt at odd moments that I was slipping down a dangerous slope.

I was drinking my after-dinner coffee in the courtyard on the Friday when Ann came across.

"I'm going to walk down to the village," she said. "I suppose you wouldn't like to come so that I can show you that picture? I mean, if you feel like it," she added nervously.

"Yes, I'd like to," I said, getting up quickly as Max Corinth headed our way.

We were half-way down the road to the village when I discovered that I'd left my handbag behind.

"I'll go," said Ann immediately, and she seemed so pleased at the idea of being of service that I let her go.

"It's a white one. I think I left it beside my chair," I called as she sped away, long legs kicking out like a colt's.

I wandered on slowly, and when she rejoined me I was standing on the first of the wooden bridges over the river, studying a sinister shadow in the water, so that I took the handbag from her without noticing it as I pointed out the object of my attention.

"Thanks, Ann. What do you think that is? Looks like a snake. Or is it just a trick of the light?"

Ann peered, and then jumped down to the bank and walked cautiously to the nearest boulder. She fished in the water and brought up a trailing weed of a peculiar rounded shape.

"Here's your snake," she said, laughing. "Gosh, this water's cold!"

And so it was that we were almost to the village before I discovered that Ann had brought the wrong handbag. It was white, like mine, but a little larger and a more expensive piece of work altogether. I was pretty sure it was Mrs Chagford's.

"Oh, I'm sorry," said Ann, dismayed. "It was on your table. At least, I'm pretty sure it was your table."

"Well, never mind. I'd better go straight back and return it. She'll be worried about it."

"Just see the picture. It's this first shop."

It was a painting of the mountain we had driven to on that first afternoon together, and it showed the glacier in the background and in the left foreground the chalet where Ann had eaten the outsize slice of Sachertorte. It was a modest work by a local artist, but the colouring was beautiful and he had captured the sunlight on the snowfield with great skill.

"Do you like it?" asked Ann.

"Very much. The mountain in a smiling mood."

I wouldn't linger, being anxious to return Mrs Chagford's handbag, and Ann came back with me. The courtyard was deserted and I went straight to the porter's desk. Franz seemed very relieved to hear my tale.

"Of course, Miss Danville. I said that was what had happened. Mrs Chagford's been in a bit of a state, I don't mind admitting. But when we searched the courtyard and found this handbag under one of the tables, I guessed what had happened. This is yours, I presume?"

"Yes."

Sleight-of-Hand

"Well, no harm done. I'll take this up to Mrs Chagford straight away."

Ann said good-night and bounded off up the stairs ahead of me, saying she had to mend a tear in her slacks. I decided to go to my room, too, and write to my father before going to bed. I had written no more than the first sentence when there was a sharp knock on the door and Mrs Chagford came in, her face cold with anger as she closed the door behind her.

"Hand them over," she said in an ugly voice I hardly recognised.

I stared at her, bewildered.

"Hand what over?"

"Don't play the innocent. Those papers you stole from my handbag."

"I haven't the slightest idea what you're talking about."

"You admit that you took my bag."

"I left my own handbag behind in the courtyard when I went down to the village after coffee. My friend came back to fetch it, and by mistake brought yours. I returned it as soon as I could. The porter had found mine in the meantime."

"You returned mine after having extracted some papers. Let's not waste time. I don't imagine you've found an opportunity of getting rid of them yet, so hand them over."

"Would you mind telling me what papers these are supposed to be?"

"You know. This play-acting's farcical. I mean to have those papers. If you don't hand them over, I shall ask the proprietor to send for the police. I shall say some money's missing, too."

"You're crazy! I assure you, Mrs Chagford, I don't know anything about these papers you're talking about."

She picked up the letter I had started and read what I had written, then snatched my handbag and turned it upside down on the bed. She had started emptying the chest of drawers before it dawned on me that she was in deadly earnest. Angrily, I caught her arm.

"This, I think, is where *I* call Mr Easher," I said.

"That would be most unwise," she said, shaking me off. "You

don't want the police brought in any more than I do, but you'll be the one in trouble. You took my bag. While it was in your possession, some valuables disappeared. I can make a good case against you, my dear, so you might as well stop playing the loyal little secretary and hand over those papers."

The contents of one drawer were strewn over the bed and she started on the next. Anger and dismay were about equally mixed in my mind. It was her word against mine, and a lot of unpleasantness, to say the least, if she took it further. I strove to keep my voice calm as I said:

"Once and for all, I know nothing about any papers."

She turned on me, her voice raised, and was in the middle of a shocking, uncontrolled tirade when the door opened and Gareth came in. I had never been so glad to see anybody as I was to see Gareth at that moment, when visions of facing police enquiries and involving Ann in the sort of inquisition that would scare her silly had me shaken. There was something about Gareth's cool look round that was immensely reassuring.

"I heard raised voices and thought you might be having trouble with Corinth again, Kate. What goes on?"

"That bitch is a scheming thief. That's what goes on," said Mrs Chagford, a look of cold fury on her face that sent Gareth's eyebrows up as he said quietly:

"You'd better explain that, Shirley. It sounds slanderous to me."

"I'll explain all right. And to the police, if she doesn't give me back what she stole. I left my bag by a table on the courtyard when I was called to the telephone this evening. Foolish of me, but I'd put it under the table and when Franz told me there was a call from New York for me, I hurried to the phone. When I got back, my bag was gone. We searched everywhere, Franz and I, but I knew it had been stolen. Then, more than an hour afterwards, if you please, Franz comes up with the tale that Miss Danville had taken it by mistake and had just returned it to him. When I opened it, I found, as I feared, some valuable papers missing."

"And what makes you think that Kate's interested in any papers of yours?"

Sleight-of-Hand

"I'll tell you, but first shall we hear from her why she kept my handbag a whole hour before returning it?"

Gareth turned to me and I hesitated. I did not want to involve Ann in any way, but could see no way of keeping her out of it. Because I felt I was creating a bad impression by my hesitation, I plunged in without more ado.

"I left my handbag under the table in the courtyard when I went off to the village. I discovered I'd left it when I was about half-way there, and Ann ran back to fetch it for me. I didn't notice at first that she'd brought the wrong bag. When I did, we came back straight away and handed it to Franz. He'd already found mine. That's all I know about it."

"A likely story. We'll see if that child corroborates it, or is she in your pay?" said Mrs Chagford.

"I won't have her brought into it," I said quickly.

"You see," said Mrs Chagford to Gareth.

"You may have to, Kate," said Gareth, sitting down on the bed.

"And before she's had time to prime her," said Mrs Chagford grimly. "We'll send for her now."

"I won't have it. I'm sorry if you've lost some papers, Mrs Chagford, but there must be some other explanation."

"You tell me, then," she said sarcastically. "They were there when I went to the telephone. Gone when you gave the bag back."

I pushed my hair back from my forehead as the thought occurred to me that perhaps Ann had swung the handbag about and the papers had dropped out.

"Were the papers in the fastened compartment of the bag or tucked in loosely?" I asked.

"What do you think? They were valuable. Look here, I've had enough of this. Either you tell me what you've done with them, or I ask Mr Easher to call the police."

Gareth crossed his legs and took out his cigarette case, saying:

"Do you mind, Kate?"

I shook my head, and he offered one to Mrs Chagford, who refused and started to turn out the next drawer.

"Shirley, let's get things a bit clearer," said Gareth. "What makes you think that Kate would want any papers of yours?"

"Her employer wants them. I'd heard that he'd lately employed an English secretary. He's sent her to do his dirty work for him."

"Her employer being where?"

"In New York, of course."

"Ever been in New York, Kate?"

"Never."

"That's what she says."

"Can we see your passport, Kate?"

I fished in my bag and handed it to him.

"No American visa. You can see for yourself, Shirley."

She looked at it and I saw a puzzled little frown pucker her forehead.

"Then someone else has hired you," she said but with less conviction.

"Listen," I said firmly. "I live and work in London, I run a little typing business, and I've just started on a writing career. I have no connections in America, and I haven't a clue about the contents of your handbag, although I'm sorry the mistake occurred. There's no more I can say to clarify it."

"I'd like to hear what the girl Ann has to say," she said obstinately.

"That I won't allow."

"Why not?"

"Because she's an immature, vulnerable girl and I see absolutely no reason to upset her by bringing her into this nasty business when she simply acted as a messenger for me."

"If I don't question her, the police will."

Gareth was prowling round the room and stopped at the door beside the wardrobe. It was a communicating door with the next room and was kept bolted.

"I think you'd better drop that bluff, Shirley," he said in a pleasant enough voice. "You don't want the police brought into this any more than we do. If you can tell us a bit more about these papers, we might be able to clear up the mystery. You thought Kate was a secretary sent to pinch some papers. They were worth money to you?"

"I've said they were valuable."

"What were they doing in your bag, then? Wouldn't a safe have been a better place?"

She was silent, pursuing her search through the dressing-table drawers now, but in a more desultory manner.

"We'll guess, then, shall we?" said Gareth gently. "Someone was willing to pay you a sum of money for some papers. The man you've been expecting, perhaps. You thought that Kate had been sent to try to get hold of them. Sent by whom? The man who had promised to pay for them, or a rival interested party?"

"Keep guessing."

"Am I warm?"

"Fairly," she said with a mocking smile, her control back.

"Your room is next door. Is that communicating door bolted on your side, too?"

"No. It was locked when I first tried it and I assumed the management kept the key."

"Then I think you've been backing the wrong horse. I rather fancy Max Corinth is your man."

She looked startled, and then her eyes narrowed as she considered this.

"Go on, Gareth," she said.

"Kate was bothered because Corinth left a guide book in her room when she was absent, and I happened to know that he was in here then for about an hour. We surmised he had a date with a chamber-maid. I saw him coming out of her room again one day in her absence, but I don't know how long he'd been in there that time. This room communicates with yours and the bolt's on this side."

"He was searching my room?"

"Seems possible."

"And he was the only other person in the courtyard this evening besides you," I said. "I remember noticing that when

Ann and I went off. Was he there when you went to the telephone?"

"Yes, he was. I suppose he could have taken my bag then."

"You don't happen to remember how long it was after Ann and I left when your telephone call came through?"

"Not accurately. About ten minutes. A bit more, perhaps."

"And how long was the telephone call?"

"About ten minutes, too. We had a slight difference of opinion," said Mrs Chagford drily.

"Ann must have turned up to fetch my bag just about that time," I said eagerly.

"A spot of luck for Corinth," said Gareth. "He summed it up quickly and was at your table handing Ann the wrong bag, delighted to delay the discovery of the theft."

Mrs Chagford was already at the door. We heard her running down the corridor.

"What's your bet that the bird's flown?" said Gareth, half smiling.

I was still too shaken to take it lightly, and began to put some of the things back in my dressing-table drawer. Mrs Chagford returned in a few minutes.

"He checked out about an hour ago," she said bitterly. "He made a telephone call, and said urgent business meant he'd have to leave at once."

"Just before I got back. He worked fast," I said.

"A professional, do you suppose?" said Gareth.

"Yes. A private detective employed by my friend," said Mrs Chagford, sounding as though she had just eaten a sour plum. "What a friend! I was a fool to trust him. I never thought he'd double-cross me. And Corinth was the last man I'd have thought was a private eye."

"A good actor," said Gareth. "It wasn't your charms, after all, Kate, that were the attraction. I take it, Shirley, that you won't attempt to bring him to justice?"

"No," she said shortly.

"Did he have the sauce to leave you a note?" asked Gareth, eyeing the envelope in her hand.

"Payment of a kind." The plum was very sour indeed.

"A lot less than you'd asked for?"

"Keep guessing. I'm going to pack. I don't intend to stay in these backwoods an hour longer than I need."

"Just a minute," said Gareth. "Don't you think you'd better apologise to Kate first?"

She eyed me coldly, then said:

"I'm sorry for the mistake, Miss Danville. Good-night."

She slammed the door and Gareth and I looked at each other.

"Well! Shall I help you straighten up?" he said, holding up my favourite peach-coloured nightdress and folding it with care.

"I feel I must have been watching a film," I said, taking it from him. "Such things don't happen to ordinary people on holiday. I must say I found Shirley Chagford a formidable proposition when roused. What do you suppose those papers were?"

"Anyone's guess. Business papers, perhaps. I believe there's a good deal of industrial espionage between rival concerns in America. Or compromising letters this man was willing to pay for either to protect himself or use against others."

"Not very nice," I said, putting back an assortment of nylons.

"No. Not nice at all. Six of one and half a dozen of the other. I'm inclined to think that our Shirley put too high a price on the papers and Mr X retaliated with a very modest sum via Max Corinth instead of coming himself with the full prize money. I can't help feeling a sneaking admiration for Corinth's acting ability. I'd have sworn he was in the film business, as he said."

"He's in an acting profession, anyway. His performance was faultless."

"Yes. I see now why he was anxious to give Castleford and me the impression that you were with him in this room when we saw him coming out. A philanderer, yes. But there must be no suspicion of anything like theft."

"And to think how he made circles round me!"

"All part of the act."

"And never mind what trouble that could have made for me."

"Well, you can't blame him for making his job as enjoyable as possible," said Gareth, grinning. "It helped his image as a dashing Don Juan, far removed from any sinister intent, and made his task much more agreeable, I'm sure. Coupled with the facts that it was you who gave him the opportunity at last of getting hold of Shirley's handbag and you who kept suspicion off him for the time he needed, I'd say you were his favourite girl to date. Time was running out for him because Shirley was beginning to lose patience at having her meeting with Mr X postponed."

"Who ever would have thought it of Max? Now if that dark Frenchman who says little and looks a lot had turned out to be a private detective, I might not have been surprised, but never in my life would I have suspected Max. Would you?"

"Of being a private detective? No. I had one or two doubts about him after that episode in your room, but not in that direction. Did he make trouble for you with John Castleford? He seemed a bit thrown that afternoon."

"John avoids trouble," I said crisply, and left it at that.

"H'm. If I'd thought any girl of mine was philandering with that wolf behind my back, there would have been trouble all right."

"John is a civilised man," I said sweetly.

"Bloodless, don't you mean?"

"You're so primitive, Gareth. Your right setting, I feel, is a stronghold in the wild Welsh mountains. The feudal system died some time ago, though, remember?"

"The man who's prepared to share his woman with others is either bloodless or a coarse brute," said Gareth, handing me the last of my scattered undergarments.

"As a matter of fact, I agree with you."

"Then that's a record."

"Don't let it go to your head."

"Afraid to yield even one inch? Where's your courage, Kate?"

"I don't underestimate the opposition."

"You don't think we might strike a balance?"

"Your idea of balance and mine are quite different, I feel."

"That's what we still have to discuss, when you're ready."

"In two weeks' time we shall be going our separate ways, Gareth."

"Not even a friendly meeting now and again?"

"Who is being unrealistic now? You know, and I know, that it's all or nothing between us. I made the choice four years ago. It still stands. It's not open to discussion."

I hoped I sounded convincing, for inside I was fighting a desperate battle against him. He was undermining my defences with every contact that we had, and I was afraid that he was clever enough to sense it, however firm my words might sound. His dark eyes met mine now and a wry little smile twisted his lips. Remember what it was like before, I reminded myself fiercely. Remember what he reduced me to. He'll do it again if I surrender, however subtly he plays down his dictatorial nature now. But the struggle was beginning to tell. Or was it the lateness of the hour and the stresses of the evening which made me feel for a fleeting moment that it was all to no avail, that he would win in the end? That it would be so easy and comforting to go into his arms then. And snap, I'd be in the trap again. My face must have betrayed something of my feelings, for he said gently:

"You're tired. It's been quite an evening, one way and another. Shirley certainly made a thorough job of turning out your belongings," he added, fishing a bra from under the bed and handing it to me.

I remembered her face as she had hurled the things out of the chest of drawers, and her voice, and the abuse. The recollection made me feel sick and shaken.

"What's the matter?" asked Gareth, as I took the bra from him and put it away.

"It was an ugly business," I said with a wobble in my voice. "I don't think I'm very good at coping with that sort of thing. Although I've been independent for four years, living in London, I begin to feel I've lived a sheltered life and don't really know much about the world."

"About the shady side of it? Why should you? It was an ugly business all right, but Corinth has gone, and Shirley will be off in

the morning. The air will be fresher for their going. Go to bed
and forget it. It was gallant but foolish of you to try to protect
your lame duck. Looked suspicious. Could have landed you in
trouble."

"Maybe. But I wasn't going to expose Ann to that woman's
tongue or involve her in such a grubby affair. She's far too young
and vulnerable. And she'd have suffered agonies of guilt about
taking the wrong handbag and getting me into a fix, even though
it wouldn't have been her fault. She has the world's biggest inferiority complex."

"Nice Kate. You wanting to protect Ann, me wanting to protect you. Where does all this protective instinct lead us in your
brave new world of independence and freedom? You can't have it
all ways, you know."

"It's far too late now to be tied in knots by your arguments."

"So it is. I'd better leave discreetly. It's half past eleven, and
people may harbour lubricious thoughts if they see me leaving
your room at this hour. Good-night, Kate. Put this business out of
your mind."

"I will. Good-night, Gareth. And ... thank you for your support. I needed it."

His eyebrows went up at this, and he smiled.

"A brave admission, wrung out of you only by your innate
honesty. Any time. You know that. And Kate," he added, putting
a hand on my shoulder, "we're none of us self-sufficient. Don't
forget that. You're not. Perhaps you got an inkling of that this
evening. And I'm not, either, whatever you may think. Sleep
well."

He slipped out of the room, leaving me to draw this bizarre
evening to a close with a second attempt to write to my father, an
attempt that failed because after all the excitement I was too tired
to collect my thoughts, and Gareth's last remarks kept buzzing in
my mind like distracting bees. Surely he was the most self-
sufficient person I had ever come across. He had wanted me only
as a shadow of himself; someone to be petted, to amuse him, to
look after his home, be a mother to his children. But the real me
he hadn't been interested in preserving, and I had never been

allowed to impinge on his chosen way of life. In fact, I doubted whether he had ever known the real me. I was only suitable material to be shaped to his chosen pattern. And he wasn't going to get the chance to use his scissors on me again, I thought grimly. But I wished he wouldn't throw down remarks that made me feel a little uneasily that I might not have known the real Gareth, either.

I put the half-written letter to my father inside my writing folder and went to bed, to dream that tiresome old dream of trying to catch a train when I'd lost my way to the station.

9

Mountain Excursion

WITH THE DEPARTURE of the two Austrian boys, Gareth yielded to Roger's request for some climbing tuition, and they spent quite a lot of time out together. I was not allowed to put Gareth out of my mind even in his absence, however, for Ann recounted most of their exploits to me at second-hand from her brother.

"Roger's fallen for your friend Mr Ferrion," she said to me one morning when we were watching two men scything hay on one of the higher alpine pastures. "Can't talk about anything else but Mr Ferrion's book, Mr Ferrion's work on the dam in Africa, Mr Ferrion's skill at climbing."

"Roger's at the hero-worshipping age."

"Well, you must admit that Mr Ferrion's got everything. Life's a bit unfair, isn't it?" she added, sighing.

"Some people do seem to have been born with all the advantages. Gareth's appeal for Roger probably has something to do with the air of authority which he carries with such ease. It appeals to adolescents. Makes them feel more secure, perhaps."

"Could be. How old is Mr Ferrion?"

"Let me see. Thirty-one."

"Have you known him a long time?"

"You could say so. We've lost touch for the past four years, though. A coincidence, our meeting here. What a pleasing picture those men make! It's interesting, watching an old skill like scything. I bet it's not as easy as it looks."

"I think he's a bit formidable, Mr Ferrion."

"I agree. The dominant male."

"Attractive, though."

"That's the danger. The hay's stacked in barns, I'm told, and brought down the mountain in the autumn by toboggan to feed the cows in the winter. They have quite a ceremony when the cows are brought down to the valley, with songs and a wreath of alpine flowers round the horns of the cow who's given the most milk during the season. I'd like to be here to see it."

"Where are the cows housed in winter, then?"

"In byres. They're individually owned."

"Life seems simpler here," said Ann.

Roger met us when we were nearly back at the hotel. He was a lively, good-looking boy with thick black hair and blue eyes. He was wearing blue jeans, a terra cotta sports shirt, and rubber-soled canvas shoes. He looked as sure-footed as a goat, coming up to us through the boulders that lined the stream.

"Hullo," I said, smiling as he reached us. "Had a good morning?"

"Super. Rock-climbing. If only I had some climbing boots we could go above the snow line, but Mother says it's not worth while buying any since we've only got three more days. Can you beat it? I could do a lot in three days."

"Well, I don't suppose Mr Ferrion wants to give the whole of his time to you, and you couldn't go on your own," said Ann.

"Why not? Anyway, I guess we've plenty of good climbs at the lower levels," said Roger, as though he was a fully fledged mountaineer now. "What a mess your neck looks," he added, eyeing his sister's red skin, which was plentifully daubed with cream.

"I know. It's jolly sore, too."

"I don't suppose you'll want to come on a trip to the Grossglockner with us tomorrow, Ann, will you? Gareth suggested we might ask you and Miss Danville to join us, but I said I didn't think you'd be keen," said Roger nonchalantly.

"Why not?" I asked.

"Oh, Ann's too shy to enjoy company. Prefers mooning about on her own. Or with you," he added politely.

"So we're on Christian name terms with our hero now, are we?" said Ann, with a grin that robbed her words of any offence.

He retaliated by baptising her with some water he scooped up from the stream. Their skirmishing concluded, I came back to the matter in hand.

"Just what does this trip entail which you are so anxious we should not join?" I asked.

"No, really, Miss Danville, it wasn't that," he said hastily, then caught my eye and grinned. "Oh, you're getting at me. Gareth suggested starting in the morning, having a picnic on the way and driving up the Grossglockner in the afternoon. It's a wonderful road up, he says. And in that super car of his it won't offer any trouble at all. But it means an early start. I don't know if it appeals to you. There could be hordes of tourists there. It's a famous spot for sightseers."

I hid a smile. He so patently did not want us to muscle in on their masculine world; I could almost see him trying to conjure up more off-putting information.

"What about it, Ann?" I asked.

She hesitated, looking at me for guidance.

"If you would like to," she said.

"We'll go," I said firmly. "Thank Gareth for the offer. What have you done with him, by the way?"

"Oh, he stopped at the hotel for a drink. We saw you on this path and he sent me up with the suggestion about tomorrow. We're starting at nine sharp."

"We'll endeavour to be punctual," I said gently, and he gave me an old-fashioned look from under his long dark lashes, then bounded off with a wave of his hand.

At fifteen, I thought, Roger Binlay showed every promise of excelling in that same male arrogance which his hero cloaked with the charm of greater experience.

The good weather which had favoured the holiday so far still held the next day, and the sun was already hot when Ann and I walked round to the parking area with the picnic basket packed for the four of us by the hotel. Gareth stowed the basket in the boot of the Mercedes and opened the door to the front passenger seat with a wicked little gleam in his eyes.

"Kate," he said, indicating the way with a gesture of his hand.

I smiled at this sop to feminine status and got in, aware of Roger's black look. To be relegated to the back with Ann when he was all agog to savour the joys of driving in the Mercedes was an insult, I could see. I would redress it after lunch but thought it would do no harm for him to take a back seat that morning. I did not realise quickly enough that Ann would bear the brunt of this unpopular arrangement, however, otherwise I might have elected to take a back seat myself from the start. As it was, Roger sulked all the morning, giving Ann terse replies to any comments she made and sometimes not bothering to respond at all, so that in the end she dried up, apart from a few remarks addressed to me. The conductor of this ill-assorted party seemed in excellent spirits, however, and I enjoyed the drive through the mountains with the Grossglockner towering above us in the distance. Gareth handled the car with expert ease. He always had, even in the old days of our engagement when it was a very ancient second-hand Alvis he had to coax along. My suggestion that he might teach me to drive had been met with an amused but firm refusal, as though the idea was in the realms of fantasy. I, of course, had submitted to his ruling with scarcely a protest.

We turned off the road up a track along a small green valley for the picnic. Food seemed to brighten Roger's outlook a little, but I could see that he thought the presence of two females had quite spoiled the excursion, as he had feared it would. Ann, anxious, as always, to mask her shyness by making herself useful, fetched and carried, and helped me wash up the dishes in a rough and ready fashion in the stream before stowing them back in the basket.

"I suggest a siesta for half an hour," said Gareth, stretching himself full length in the dappled shade of a larch tree.

I propped myself up against the trunk and took my notebook out of my bag.

"Got your camera, Ann?" asked Roger.

"No, I've used up the film."

"Well, you could have bought another in the village."

"The holiday's nearly over."

"You were too mean to fork out for it, I suppose. Never known anybody as tight-fisted as Ann. Hasn't spent a bean for the past two weeks. What are you going to do with all that money?" he asked sarcastically.

Ann flushed scarlet, then stooped to fasten the buckle of her sandal without saying anything. Roger looked at her, then said witheringly:

"Oh, you're so *wet*."

He was obviously venting his disappointment in the excursion on Ann and I was angry with him but before I could say anything, Gareth stood up, saying:

"I want a map from the car. Come with me, Roger."

Ann murmured something about looking for wild flowers and went off up the valley. I could see Gareth standing by the bonnet of the car, obviously tearing a strip off Roger, who was moodily kicking a tuft of grass at his feet. I was glad Gareth had tackled him. He would do it far more effectively than I. When they came back, Roger's face was red and he avoided my eyes, walking off in the direction Ann had taken with an expression on his face which suggested that the apology would not be exactly a gracious one. Gareth had sat down again and opened the map out on the grass beside him.

"Thank you for doing that," I said. "It was needed."

"M'm. He wants taking in hand. A nice lad basically, but a doting mother and a too-occupied father don't exactly bring out the best in him."

"And he learns how to bait Ann from his mother, I'm afraid. Boys are cruel. You expect that. But from a woman, it's inexcusable."

"Ann will have to learn to fight her own battles."

"She will. She's only eighteen."

He studied his map and I returned to my notes. Presently he said:

"They're coming back. In the front again with me, Kate, for the rest of the day."

"He'll be terribly disappointed. Won't you relent if he's made amends?"

"He'll stay in the back today. There'll be other opportunities before he leaves, if he behaves himself for the rest of today.

Anyway," he added with a grin, "I believe in keeping kids in their place."

"And females of all ages?" I asked meekly.

"That is something we still have to discuss."

I gave him a measuring glance. In lean-cut grey whipcord trousers, white shirt and flowing grey and blue striped tie, he looked much fitter than when I had first seen him at the hotel. Deeply tanned, with no hint of sallowness now, he had lost the look of strain about the eyes, and lay back in the grass surveying me lazily. But even then, lounging and relaxed, there was a sense of smouldering intensity beneath the surface, like a tiger in the sun who could pounce with lightning speed if any prey came within reach. In ten days' time, I thought, this dangerous interlude will have come to an end.

Ann came back without any flowers but looking happier. Roger bore the expression of a brave martyr. He flashed a look of indignant protest at Gareth when the latter made it plain that the same stations were to be kept in the car, but Gareth's face was implacable. You won't budge him with any appeals, my boy, I said to myself. As well try to soften granite. Jove has spoken.

I took my place beside Gareth and we set off. The scenery was magnificent, the atmosphere in the back of the car polite without being exactly vivacious, while in the front, Gareth was obviously enjoying the concentrated driving across mountain passes and I enjoyed the grandeur of the mountains and tried to identify them from the map for the benefit of the young people behind. There were a good many cars travelling up the magnificently engineered hair-pin bends of the Glockner road, but when we reached the highest spot and got out to see the glaciers and snows of the Grossglockner Massif all about us, cars and people were dwarfed by the surroundings and we were thrilled by the sheer majesty of it all.

At those heights, the air was bitingly cold off the glaciers and we were glad of tea in a refreshment hut near the Parkplatz. Afterwards, Roger and Gareth walked off on their own a little way to another viewpoint where Gareth appeared to be pointing out climbing routes. As they came back to the car, I saw Gareth laugh and ruffle Roger's hair, and guessed that they had come to terms. But Roger still had to go in the back with Ann. As Gareth held the rear door open for him, the boy gave him a half humorous, half rueful look accompanied by a little shrug of the shoulders that said much. If we have to have these tiresome females, well, I'll try to bear it with as good a grace as possible, but the whole thing would have been so much better confined to the superior male world, was how I read it. Two of a kind there, I thought darkly, and found myself in a decidedly independent frame of mind for the rest of the excursion.

Back at the hotel car park, Gareth had the bonnet of the Mercedes up, explaining something to Roger beside him. Ann was struggling with the picnic basket. I gave her a hand, saying thank you to Gareth for the day.

"We enjoyed it immensely, Ann and I. Thank you so much for the privilege of joining the men. I hope we didn't cramp your style too much."

Gareth straightened up and gave me one of his broody looks.

"The pleasure, Kate, was all ours. Leave the basket. Roger and I will bring it."

"We can manage it," I said cheerfully. "We'll leave you and Roger to your engineering class."

"Thank you very much, Mr Ferrion," said Ann with a shy smile as we left them.

I had to go back a few minutes later to fetch my sun-glasses which I'd left in the car. Gareth saw me coming and said something to Roger which sent that lad off in the direction of the hotel with a friendly wave to me.

"I left my sun-glasses in the side pocket of the car," I said.

Gareth reached in and fished them out. He held them in his hands thoughtfully for a moment.

"Did I detect a little flag-waving just now?" he asked.

"Perhaps."

"Still necessary between us?"

"Indeed, yes. I must remind you, in case you forget."

Mountain Excursion

"You think I'm in danger of forgetting?"

"I think it would please you to see my flag hauled down."

"In one respect. Two flags *can* fly side by side, you know."

"Without getting tangled up?"

"With a little care, yes."

"Don't you mean one under the other?" I said, holding out my hand for the sun-glasses.

"Well, shall we have a debate about that?"

I shook my head.

"It's been debated before, and the vote taken."

"It's not been debated before. That's my point. Afraid, Kate?"

I was pinned against the car, since he was leaning on it with one arm on each side of me. There was something in Gareth that I was afraid of. That I had always been afraid of. A ruthlessness in him, a power to bend me to his will, which was why I could not afford to give him an inch. I spoke quietly, controlling only with effort the shakiness which threatened my voice.

"Listen, Gareth. I don't know why you're anxious to renew that old debate which was finished years ago. We were in love, yes. But we didn't love each other. There's a difference. We didn't even know each other. Or if you thought you knew me, it was only a child fashioned to your mould. I ended up without a mind or a will of my own, a puppet dancing to your tune; and you ended up by treating me as the doormat I'd become. I was young, quite immature; you were riding on the crest of a physical conquest which pleased you. In the end, even I, infatuated as I was, couldn't blind myself to the arrogance of your treatment which was reducing me to a nobody. But I told you all this in that letter. What is the point of going over it all again now? I've grown up. I'm not the same Kate that you conquered."

"I didn't suggest that you were, or that I wanted you to be. I merely wanted to answer that letter."

"There was no answer," I said passionately.

"There was and there is."

"Then I'm not interested any more."

"You're afraid. I wonder why? Perhaps you haven't grown up

quite enough, Kate," he said, and, taking my face between his hands, he kissed me gently before releasing me. "Don't take too long, my love. I'm not that patient," he added, then handed me the sun-glasses and walked off, leaving me staring after him in bewilderment.

10

Monsieur Corbeil

SITTING IN THE courtyard by the fountain, sipping a mid-morning cup of coffee, I watched the dancing drops of water as they fell into the stone basin below, feeling troubled and restless. I had slept badly the previous night and woke with a headache which still persisted. I had arranged to drive the Binlays to Innsbruck and see them off, and we were leaving at noon. Meanwhile, I had the courtyard to myself, and I was pondering on the way this holiday had turned out. I had expected a peaceful interlude when I could get my next book plotted and perhaps started, an interlude which would end in my decision to marry John and look forward to a well organised, satisfying life together. Instead, that grey car which had shattered my peace on the very first morning of my approach to Mölden had continued its destructive work, pushing John out of my life, making any worthwhile work on my book impossible, destroying my ease of mind, putting all my cut and dried plans into confusion, and eroding the confidence which it had taken so many years to build. I should have fled as soon as I saw him, I thought. Made some excuse. But I had booked the room for a month and it wouldn't have been easy. By what devil's work had he turned up here?

"Pardon, mademoiselle."

It was Monsieur Corbeil, the stolid swarthy man who sat so often by himself with his paper and glass of cognac, and with whom I had exchanged no more than a "Good-morning" or "Good-evening" ever since I had arrived. He seemed to like being an observer of the scene rather than a participator. Balancing a cup of coffee in one hand, he reached for the paper and the cigarette packet which he had left on the chair opposite me and which I had not noticed.

"Oh, I'm sorry, Monsieur Corbeil. Have I taken your table?"

"Of course not. It is pleasant here, by the little fountain, is it not?"

"Indeed. Won't you share it, then?"

"You looked deep in thought. Perhaps I shall intrude."

"Thoughts I shall be quite glad to put aside," I said with a smile, for I rather liked the look of this man with the heavy-lidded dark eyes and the sardonic but tolerant expression that reminded me a little of my father.

"Then in that case, thank you." He sat down and gave me a quirky smile. "I, too, shall be glad to postpone reading the newspaper. Dismal stuff on holiday. The world grows ever more foolish, it seems. We would do better to cultivate our own gardens and ignore it."

"I agree. Easy to forget the rest of the world in a spot as lovely as this."

"But not easy to forget oneself, perhaps. Forgive me. You looked worried just now. Holidays can give one too much time to think, perhaps."

"How long are you staying, Monsieur Corbeil?"

"Another week, and then on to Italy. An enforced retirement after illness is giving me a chance to travel in a leisurely manner again."

"I hope you're feeling better for it."

He shrugged his shoulders.

"Ça va. But you, Miss Danville. You are enjoying yourself? Getting material for a book, perhaps. I heard that you were a writer."

"Starting to be. Only one book published so far. A second due out in the autumn."

"An honourable calling. I am a journalist, so we have a common craft. Tell me about your work. You smoke?"

"No, thank you."

We talked for the next half hour about the craft of writing, or rather he talked and I for the most part listened, for he obviously knew far more than I and was an absorbing talker on his subject. When I thanked him for his advice, he said:

"It is not necessary to thank me. Few things are more pleasant and flattering to a middle-aged man than advising youth on a craft dear to him. Besides, it is always enjoyable to—what do you say?—talk shop."

"It is indeed."

"We must do it again. Good, too, for banishing troublesome thoughts. Many people envy the young. Not for the world would I go back to suffer the pangs of the heart that youth endures."

"You've no advice to offer in that direction, then?" I said, half laughing.

"Only a pair of willing ears. Sometimes, that helps. But I am a sceptic and my advice on such matters would, I fear, not be welcome."

"I'm not so sure. I feel the need of some bracing scepticism just now. My father provides it for me as a rule."

"Then by all means let me stand in for your father. It is so easy for a looker-on to be a philosopher. What problem have you for Socrates?"

"When I came away, I had my life well under control. My future looked untroubled and satisfying, and I felt sure of myself and my aims. And here, it's all come to pieces. Been shattered by an encounter I never expected. The question I'll put to you is, when I get back home, will the old pattern reassert itself?"

"That depends on the nature of the explosion," he said slowly, "but the odds are against it. What is the saying? You can never swim in the same water twice. The immutable law of change is always at work. This explosion. It has made so much difference?"

"Yes. Even people no longer seem the same," I said unhappily, thinking how John, somehow, had been reduced to a cardboard character. "How can one have confidence in oneself, in one's plans, when they can be blown sky high so quickly?"

"Perhaps they were never of fundamental importance to you."

"They were. They concerned freedom."

"Oh, we are in deep waters there, Miss Danville. There are so many aspects of freedom. You were thinking, perhaps, of freedom from the tyranny of personal affections?"

"Of deep personal involvements, yes."

"Always more difficult for women, but are any of us really free? Freedom from personal involvement for what? Define your problem, and you see it more clearly."

"Freedom to be an individual, I suppose."

"And now you see that threatened?"

"Yes."

"Forgive me. You may not wish to be personal. But it is the dark young man who is the threat?"

I was surprised. I had spent little time with Gareth. To an outsider, I would have thought my link appeared to be with John Castleford, if anybody.

"What makes you think that?" I asked.

He shrugged his shoulders with a little smile.

"There is a current between you two. Not apparent perhaps to people with lives of their own to concentrate on, but I am a looker-on with no life of my own to occupy my thoughts. I have retired from life, you might say. And so I notice others. When he looks at you, it is all there, in his eyes. And in yours, too. He is unusual, that one."

"Very," I said drily.

"You have known him long?"

"We were engaged when I was twenty; it was broken off after a year."

"By you?"

"There was a frightful row. But I was the one who ran away and wouldn't see him again. I had to escape. I'd become a puppet, completely dominated by him. I had to find myself."

"And the meeting here was chance?"

"As far as I know."

"Why did you not run again, then, if you felt threatened?"

"That is the question I've been asking myself."

"You are afraid that your new found self will crumble again?"

"If I don't watch out."

"I think you may be over cautious there. You should have more confidence in yourself. You are a writer. You have work to do. You are a person in your own right. To think that that could be destroyed is to under-estimate your own strength of mind, and perhaps the intelligence of the man in question. He is no fool, that one. And only a fool would want to crush a personality like yours."

"You don't know how domineering he is. There's power there."

"Obviously. He mis-used it in the past?"

I hesitated, trying to be completely honest.

"Yes, but I had fallen so flat on my face before him that I must have tempted him to do so."

"Men are by nature selfish with their women. They need no encouragement. And now he wants to renew the engagement?"

"I don't know. He wants to answer the letter I sent him when I ran away."

"And you don't wish that?"

"I'm afraid to give him an inch for fear of being back where I was five years ago."

"I repeat, you under-estimate yourself. You forget that the years have brought changes to you, and to him. Time does that. You have nothing to fear if your mind is clear."

"If only it were just a question of minds!" I said despairingly, but this evoked a throaty chuckle from my companion which brought a reluctant smile to my lips, too.

"What an admission!" he said. "Heresy. But you were trying to say, perhaps, that if only the senses and the mind would run together in unison, there would be no problem. Alas, so often the mind and the body are in conflict. I should not be smoking this cigarette if it were otherwise. The solution of satisfying the one without the other is not possible for you, perhaps?"

"Gareth is an all-or-nothing man where I'm concerned, I fancy. And it wouldn't be possible for me, either. There was never anything ... frivolous about our relationship. And middle-class family traditions hold good with us still."

"So," he said thoughtfully, and I wondered whether he saw us as exceptions to the permissive English society he had read about or whether he was knowledgeable enough to know that permissiveness was confined to a much smaller section of the English community than might be thought from report. If it had ever entered my head to suggest any temporary liaison with Gareth, I really believe he would have beaten me. To Monsieur Corbeil, perhaps, this was illogical.

"But I mustn't take up any more of your time with my problems. Thank you for listening so patiently. In the end, I've got to work it out myself. But it's not the holiday I expected," I added with a rueful smile.

"And things won't ever be the same again, which is a pity when you'd got it all sorted out so nicely. That is life," he said with a humorous shrug.

"And a very tricky business it is."

"I wonder if it seems as tricky to our shy English spinster," he said as the grey-haired lady crossed to the table furthest away from us, coffee cup in one hand and a book in the other.

She merged with the shade of the tree as I looked at her.

"She's very elusive. I don't think she's spoken to anybody since she's been here. In fact, I've hardly noticed her, and yet she's been here ever since I arrived, I believe. I seem to remember seeing her that first day," I concluded, thinking back. It seemed a long time ago.

"Yes. She arrived with me the day before you came. Her name is Miss Courtland. That is all I know. Very shy and nervous, I'd say."

"She has rather a sweet face. More people are handicapped by shyness than we realise," I added as Ann came out wearing a light coat and carrying gloves, obviously ready to go. She smiled at me and seemed to hesitate as she saw my companion.

Monsieur Corbeil rose then and said with a little bow:

"I've enjoyed our talk, Miss Danville."

"Kate."

"A good English name. Kate. We will talk again, I hope. Now I must go to the village before lunch."

He smiled and left me, and Ann ran across.

Monsieur Corbeil

"I just wanted a word with you before the others come. To say thank you for making this such a super holiday for me," she said awkwardly. "I'd dreaded it, and it's been the best holiday I've ever had. You've been so kind."

"I've enjoyed your company, Ann. We'll meet again soon."

"I've scribbled our address on this piece of paper. Just in case. If it wouldn't be an awful bore and you should happen to be anywhere near . . ." her voice trailed off, her eyes unhappy as she looked away.

"It won't be a bore, and I don't intend to lose touch. You've got my address and telephone number. Mind you use it. I shall be disappointed if you don't. It will be easy to meet in London. What about fixing a day for lunch now?" I added, for I could see that she expected me to fade out of her life. Ann Binlay had learned to expect very little from people.

Her eyes brightened and she fumbled in her bag for her diary. We fixed a day in early August and I told her to come to the office for me. Her gratitude made me feel guilty, as it often did. Before we could say any more, her mother and Roger joined us.

"There you are, Ann. I've been looking for you. Have you labelled your case and put it outside your room for the porter?"

"I've labelled it but I haven't put it outside. I can carry it down."

"That's what the porter's for, my dear. Go and put it out, and for heaven's sake do something to take the shine off your nose. It's like a beacon."

As Ann ran off, Roger handed me a book.

"Mr Ferrion asked me to pass this on to you when I'd finished it."

"Thanks," I said, and went round to the parking place to fetch my car. I would have been pleased if Mrs Binlay had been forced to walk to Innsbruck carrying her own luggage, but since her cases were so large that we had difficulty in stowing them away in the boot of my car, the idea was hardly practicable. Ann finished up with her suitcase on her lap. I wondered whether Mrs Binlay realised that she was destroying every shred of that girl's confidence. Why was she so cruel? Jealous of the first wife's child?

Jealous of her husband's affection for his daughter? Or was it just the shallow irritation of a pretty, very feminine woman with a plain, untalented girl in her charge? I couldn't tell, but I disliked her very much as she sat beside me, chatting so charmingly, while I drove to Innsbruck.

There was no time after I had seen them off to get back to the hotel for lunch, and I found a pleasant little café in Innsbruck, carrying with me the picture of Ann's toothy farewell smile and waving handkerchief. Because something about her wrenched at my heart and because there was little I could do about it but keep in touch with her, I opened Gareth's book over my lunch and read the first chapter. His style was good; clear and terse, as I would have expected, but unexpectedly eloquent about Brunel's work. The illustrations were superb and I, a complete ignoramus about engineering and quite incurious about it as long as it worked, found myself falling under the spell of his enthusiasm. I hadn't realised how deeply he was committed to his profession.

When I arrived back at the hotel, Franz handed me a large, flat parcel.

"Miss Binlay asked me to give this to you, Miss Danville," he said with a smile. "But not until she had gone."

I thanked him and carried it up to my room. When I unwrapped it, I found the painting of the mountain which she had been so anxious to show me that evening. On the back she had scrawled: With love from Ann. So that was why she had been saving her money, to Roger's disgust. Touched, I sat down straight away to write and thank her.

11

A little Star-shine

IT WAS NEARLY four o'clock by the time I had finished writing to Ann, and I decided to stay and have a pot of tea before going out again. The hotel was quiet. Everybody was out, it seemed, except one solitary figure in the courtyard below. Miss Courtland was sitting at the table near the fountain, book open beside the teapot. She was wearing a pink and grey print dress. As I watched, she took off her spectacles and put them in the case, closing her book. I saw her move her hand over her eyes, as though they were tired, and then she poured out her tea. The shadowy pattern of the mountain ash tree on the gravel surface below scarcely moved on that warm, still day. The geraniums blazed, the fountain glittered. The empty tables made their own bright pattern. And that small grey-haired figure looked very lonely.

I ordered a pot of tea from Franz and went out into the courtyard. Miss Courtland looked up with a diffident little smile when I said:

"Hullo. May I join you?"

"Please do. It's so pleasant here, isn't it? I spend a lot of time here."

She was younger than I had thought. In her early fifties, perhaps. The grey eyes seemed too large for the small, pale face. Her voice was quiet and gentle. I glanced at the book she had been reading.

"You like poetry?" I observed.

"Yes. I find it so comforting and reassuring. Of course," she added apologetically, "only the poets of the past. I can't understand modern poetry. I'm afraid I seek for hope, not despair."

"And a very healthy aim, too. Who are your favourites?"

"Well, just at the moment, I am enjoying Robert Louis Stevenson, a new discovery for me. He has such a robust, adventurous spirit, and I suppose that appeals to me because my life has been the opposite of adventurous. In fact, this holiday on my own is about the most adventurous thing I've ever done in my life."

"I hope it's come up to expectation."

"Oh yes, it's beautiful here. And we've had such lovely weather. I was very nervous about coming on my own, but it was so much easier than I thought."

"It always is."

"I expect you think me very foolish. A woman of my age afraid to travel alone when mere children go off to all parts of the world without a qualm."

"Of course I don't think you're foolish. Times have changed so quickly. I haven't travelled much myself, yet."

"But you are young, and so competent, like all the young people today, it seems. I envy them their opportunities. No, not envy. That's an ugly word. I just wish I'd been born thirty years later, but then I'd probably have been just as timid and ineffectual. Now that I've taken the plunge and come away on my own, though, I shall make myself do it again."

My tea arrived and as I busied myself with it, I asked her how long she still had here.

"I go home tomorrow. My father is arriving home on Monday from a visit to America, and I must be back before then."

"Haven't you found it a little lonely here?"

"I'm used to being on my own. And one is never lonely with books to keep one company. As a matter of fact, I really prefer it that way, because I'm not good at being sociable. I can't talk to strangers, as a rule. But I can, to you. You have such a friendly, sympathetic manner."

"Thank you," I said, smiling.

"And it's interesting, watching you all. So busy, so active," she said wistfully.

We talked about the surrounding country, or rather, I talked and she encouraged me with the odd question. She was keenly interested, and it dawned on me that she had in fact been no farther than the village and the hill at the back of the hotel. And today was her last day.

"Would you like a drive with me into the mountains? We've nearly three hours before dinner," I said.

She accepted with an innocent pleasure that reminded me of Ann, and her enjoyment of that tour, which took in a high mountain pass, was reward enough for another afternoon of missed work.

"There's a special celebration at the village beer garden this evening, Miss Courtland," I said as we arrived back at the hotel. "Folk songs and dancing. How about rounding off your holiday by coming with me?"

"It sounds a lovely idea. A beer garden. Would it be all right? On our own, I mean."

"Would you like me to rustle up a man? I dare say Monsieur Corbeil would be agreeable."

"Oh no. Not at all. I'd sooner we went on our own, if that will be all right. I'm stupid with men. Never know what to say to them. I should feel a dead weight."

"I agree that it's nice to be rid of them sometimes," I said cheerfully. "We'll go on our own."

I had left little time to change for dinner. Gareth, late back from another day on the mountains, was waiting outside the bathroom door when I emerged.

"You look eighteen again," he observed, his eyes dancing. "All dewy-eyed and fresh and shining. Can I date you for this evening?"

"I'm already booked."

"Dashed again. Who with?"

"Miss Courtland."

"Come again."

"The quiet lady who sits in the corner of the dining-room by that revolting potted plant."

"What high jinks are you two going to indulge in?"

"Nothing more dangerous than an hour or two in the beer garden."

"Can't I come, too?"

"Sorry. She's frightened of men. I'm not joking, Gareth. She really is. Terribly shy. And do you know, she's been here three weeks and not spoken to a soul, and not a soul has spoken to her until I had tea with her here today. And she made a terrific effort to be brave enough to come on holiday abroad by herself, but she's seen nothing of the country. So I thought we'd have a little celebration together this evening. She leaves tomorrow."

I was whispering, for fear of being overheard, but we were alone in the little alcove which led to the bathroom.

"And I'd spoil it? Even if I put on my most beguiling manner?"

"Even your great charm would only petrify her. I know what would happen. She'd be dumb and we'd be trying too hard, and it just wouldn't come off."

"Perhaps you're right. Three's an awkward number, anyway. Enjoy yourselves. Dear Kate. So warm-hearted to everybody else; so hard-hearted to me. You smell nice. What is it? Mémoire Chérie?" he said wickedly, looking at the tin of talcum powder in my hand.

"Gardenia," I said, and fled. I knew Gareth in that mood. Utterly unmanageable. But he had been understanding about it. Time was when he would have overruled me with a laugh and a hug and taken charge of the evening. Perhaps the years had changed Gareth, too. If so ... But I dismissed this dangerous trend of thought and concentrated on getting down to dinner on time.

The evening proved a great success. Miss Courtland was delighted with the dancers in their colourful Tyrolean dress, and with a glass of lager to encourage her she joined in the choruses of some of the songs. She had a good knowledge of German, I found, and her happy response to the gaiety of the evening surprised me and gave me an inkling of the charming eager young Miss Courtland who had somehow faded into this timid, gentle, elderly spinster. What had her life been to have drained her of all colour and driven her into a solitary world of her own? Her tongue loosened by a second glass of lager towards the end of the evening, she enlightened me a little.

"I don't know that I should have a second glass," she said apologetically, as the waiter arrived with it and presented it with a flourish, "but that singing has made me thirsty. I used to enjoy choral singing when I was young. A wonderful escape."

"From what?"

"A life I hated. A prison," she said simply, looking into her glass as though she saw it all there.

"I'm sorry."

"Oh, you mustn't be. I suppose a lot of people would think I'd been very fortunate. In any case, I don't believe in self-pity. We experience only what we are. I'm a feeble person. Never able to stand up for myself. I have only myself to blame. But I refuse to introduce a depressing note into this happy evening. In any case, the bitterness has all gone now. The years bring acceptance, and their own compensations. I have a niece who is very dear to me. She's happily married now and I'm godmother to her little son. And it was Dinah who gave me my dog, Barrie. A golden cocker spaniel. You have no idea what a delightful companion he is."

"You live alone?"

"Oh no. Although, in a sense, yes. I manage the house for my father. He's Andrew Courtland, creator of Courtland Enterprises, a large business empire. Perhaps you've heard of it."

"Yes, I have."

"He's in his eighties now, Father, but although he says he's half retired, leaving it to the young ones, he still keeps his hands on the reins. Still loves power. He won't give it up until he dies. And in a way, I think, it keeps him alive."

"He must be a brilliant man."

"Yes. So charming, too, with a deceptively gentle manner. And utterly ruthless underneath with a computer instead of a heart. I was always frightened of him, even when I was a child and my mother stood between us. When she died I tried to escape, but he somehow persuaded me to stay. A quiet intimidation, you might say. We've always entertained a lot—business entertaining. And I was trained to supervise the housekeeping, keep the servants happy and hire the services of outside caterers when necessary. So you see, I never had to work myself. Only see that it was all organised efficiently so that my father couldn't fault anything in his handsome country home. I've never wanted for money. Only for affection. My father isn't aware of my existence as a human being."

"But you must have met a lot of interesting people."

"I've never been a good mixer. Father makes up for that. I've always been kept in the background, to oil the wheels. And I used to think that one day I'd escape, but I never have. You know how it goes:

> Tomorrow you will live you always cry;
> In what far country does this morrow lie?

I often think of those lines."

"It's never too late."

"At fifty-two? But how wrong of me to be talking like this when I've just enjoyed a lovely holiday! It's only that somehow, looking at you young people, I feel I've missed so much. To love and be loved is the greatest happiness of existence, Sydney Smith so truly said. For a woman to miss that—well, it seems in a way a wasted life."

"There are other satisfactions. You have years before you in which to travel, enjoy books, music."

"Of course," she said cheerfully. "Forgive me for looking back when the present is so delightful. Really, I haven't had such a jolly evening for years and years. It all reminds me of a musical show I once saw in London. *White Horse Inn.* Before your time, but very charming."

"It *is* rather like a musical comedy," I said, looking around as another chorus set the visitors joining in merrily over their tankards of beer.

Miss Courtland spoke no more of the past, but talked a lot about her dog, who obviously filled her need for someone to love. I wondered if she would ever come abroad again on her own. I doubted it. In spite of her brave assurances, she had only exchanged one lonely setting for another, and had been almost as

A Little Star-shine

restricted here as she was at home. Miss Courtland, I thought, belonged to the defeated. Another victim of male domination. But perhaps born with a gentle spirit doomed to defeat in our rough world, anyway.

I was grateful to the moon for shining that night and bestowing a magic beauty on the mountains around us as we walked back. I wanted everything to be perfection for Miss Courtland's last evening. She had elected to walk rather than be driven when I had asked her to choose. "Such a beautiful walk, and I'm still a good walker. I get a lot of practice," she had said.

We stopped on the little bridge across the river and admired the wavering reflection of the moon in the water. If I could, I would have whistled up nightingales for Miss Courtland, but the sound of the water and the soft murmur of the pines made their own pleasant song. We talked about poetry and the countryside, and were in such an uplifted, uninhibited mood that we walked up the track to the hotel singing "Over the sea to Skye", Miss Courtland in a thin true soprano, myself an octave lower and my pitch less true.

> "Sing me a song of a lad that is gone,
>   Say, could that lad be I?
>   Merry of soul he sailed on a day
>   Over the sea to Skye."

chirped Miss Courtland to the amazement of Gareth, who, coming round from the car park of the hotel, met us at the entrance to the courtyard. Without hesitation, however, he took up the challenge, and to Miss Courtland's fluty voice added his own quite good baritone. Was there anyone with Welsh blood in his veins who couldn't sing, I thought, as thus reinforced, the song rang out:

> "Give me again all that was there,
>   Give me the sun that shone!
>   Give me the eyes, give me the soul,
>   Give me the lad that's gone!"

Gareth had linked arms with us, one on either side of him, and conducted us across the courtyard as we sang the last verse:

> "Billow and breeze, islands and seas,
>   Mountains of rain and sun,
>   All that was good, all that was fair,
>   All that was me is gone."

And as we sang the last chorus, he released us by a table, then said gravely:

"And now, ladies, don't you think I'd better order some tea or coffee to sober you down?"

"An excellent idea," I said, sitting down.

"Oh dear," gasped Miss Courtland, laughing. "It's Mr Ferrion, isn't it? What must you think of us? I assure you that if we're intoxicated, it is only with enjoyment. We've had such a delightful evening in the beer garden. And how well you sing!"

"I should have been with you, evidently," he said with a smile. "Now, shall it be tea or coffee?"

"Oh, that *is* kind. I really should be packing. But yes, tea would be splendid to round off the evening. The courtyard is so pretty at night with the lanterns, and it really is beautifully mild."

Gareth ordered the tea, and Miss Courtland, her inhibitions obviously vanquished for that evening, showed every sign of enjoying his company. He struck just the right note with her: a little gentle teasing and a kindly deference. He was probably showing me how lamb-like he could be, but my heart warmed to him for taking the trouble to round off her evening so happily.

When she said good-night, her voice was tremulous.

"I shall never forget this evening. Nor this little courtyard," she added, looking round it. "Nor you, Miss Danville. I've never come home singing in my life before. Star-shine at night. Something I never expected to experience at my time of life. Thank you for conjuring it up, my dear."

And then, as though confused by this display of feeling, she murmured a quick "good-night, and thank you again," and slipped away.

A Little Star-shine

"Well, well," said Gareth, sitting down and taking out his cigarettes. "Will that pot stretch to another cup?"

"Just about."

"Star-shine at night. I don't get the reference."

"Her favourite poet just now. Robert Louis Stevenson.

'I will make you brooches and toys for your delight
Of bird-song at morning and star-shine at night.' "

"Of course. How does it go on? Something about blue days at sea. Do you know the rest of it?"

"More or less."

"Say it, Kate. You've a nice voice for verse."

I passed him his tea and searched my memory.

" 'I will make a palace fit for you and me
Of green days in forests and blue days at sea.
I will make my kitchen, and you shall keep your room,
Where white flows the river and bright blows the broom,
And you shall wash your linen and keep your body white
In rainfall at morning and dewfall at night.'

I can't remember the rest."

"I'm in a very marsh-mallow mood tonight, so such romantic sentiments appeal. The evening's been a smash-hit, I gather."

"M'm. I'm sorry Miss Courtland's going tomorrow, and that I didn't get to know her before. After tomorrow, there will only be three left of the original number when I arrived. An odd assortment. Funny how well you feel you know them after such brief encounters."

"You get a sort of clannish feeling in a small hotel. The newcomers seem almost interlopers after a time."

I thought of Max Corinth and Mrs Chagford; the Binlays; Miss Courtland; Monsieur Corbeil. I seemed to have learned a little more of life from all of them. There was something about this holiday, these new encounters, that was changing me; not so much changing but cracking the crust of busy-ness which I seemed to have wrapped round me of recent years. And the prime cracker, of course, was opposite, sipping his tea and studying me with a thoughtful expression. I wondered how he was managing to spin his currency allowance out for four weeks, and just how and why he had hit on this hotel at this time, but I wasn't going to ask any personal questions. That road was too dangerous. Less than a week to go, and what then? Would this all seem like a dream, with perhaps only Ann's eager face to remind me now and again? I couldn't see into the future at all. I only knew I was a different person from that complacent, well-ordered Kate Danville who had driven up the road three weeks before and been passed by a scorching Mercedes.

"It's been quite a day," I said, getting up. "I'm for bed. Goodnight, Gareth. And thank you for the tea. And the baritone. I liked it, too."

"We might try a duet one day."

"Your voice would drown mine."

"You're too modest."

But I was too tired to take up battle stations with Gareth that night, and I smiled and left him.

12

Visitor from the Past

IF GARETH HAD felt in a marsh-mallow mood the previous evening, his mood the next day resembled a hard and very sour green apple. I met him on his way to the car park as I returned from my morning walk, and his grim expression made me say:

"Is anything the matter?"

"A new arrival. A mutual acquaintance. Janet Renton."

"Janet? Not another coincidence!"

"I doubt it."

"You don't seem pleased about it."

"I'm not. Janet Renton is not my favourite character."

"The sister of your oldest friend?"

"That's irrelevant."

"Did she know you were here?"

"Ian must have told her."

"Is that surprising?"

"Yes, considering Janet lives and works in London and Ian's working in Heidelberg."

"I don't see why you're so angry. Janet's a nice enough person and I don't see that she'll interfere with you."

"No? You never were a good judge of character, Kate. Easily taken in. Janet Renton's a troublemaker. She did some hatchet work on us, remember? To have her here now is about as pleasant a prospect as a wet week. I hope to goodness she's not staying long. Find out and let me know, will you?"

"Can't you ask her yourself?"

"I intend to be very scarce while she's here. You and she will no doubt enjoy being buddies," he added bitingly.

"If you greeted her this morning with that expression, I imagine that the less she sees of you, the better she'll be pleased."

"I did not greet her this morning. Luckily I spotted her arrival before she saw me and I took appropriate avoiding action. And you disappoint me, Kate. You really do. Can you still be so blind?"

I was nettled by his ironic expression, and said briskly:

"I lack your keen penetration, no doubt, and also your intolerance."

"Well, I'm off for the day. Happy chatting," he said so savagely that I stared after him in amazement.

He shot off in the Mercedes a few minutes later, driving much too fast, and I made my way to my room. Looking down into the courtyard, I could see Janet sitting at a table on the far side, looking round her with interest, a cup of coffee in front of her. She hadn't changed much in the four years since I had last seen her. Tall, with sand-coloured hair and bold features, she was a few years older than I was. I had always liked her well articulated Scottish voice. She was a physiotherapist in some municipal clinic when I last had contact with her.

The memory of that last meeting stirred now like a sharp probe in an old wound. The information she had given me about Gareth and his secretary had stunned me at first, then acted as the final thrust to action. I had realised for months past that Gareth had reduced me to a puppet, dancing to his tune, so that I would make no decision without recourse to him, and indeed seemed incapable of any independent action at all. Looking back now, I was amazed at the extent of his domination. I gave up my friends, my interests, my chance of a better job, my efforts to write, just to be with him whenever he was free, accepting his decisions, holding my life at his disposal. He had only to lift a finger, and I came running. In his arms, any disposition to argue sank like a stone. Masterful, with an irresistible magnetism for me, Gareth drove me as he drove his car. But whether I should have found the courage to break and run if it had not been for the events of that last week-end and Janet's news, I still couldn't say. Gareth's powers of persuasion at that time were enormous. And so in a way, I thought, I had reason to be grateful to Janet, for I had found myself during these past years of freedom; I was an individual again with some measure of self-confidence and self-respect, and the clock could not be put back.

When I went out to the courtyard to join Janet, she looked both astonished and dismayed to see me. She quickly wiped off the expression of dismay, but not before I had recognised it too clearly to be able to put it down to imagination on my part.

"Hullo, Janet," I said. "This is a surprise."

"You're telling me! Join me in a coffee and tell me what you're up to, in the same hotel as Gareth after all this time."

She spoke jokingly, but her eyes were alert, hostile almost. I spoke in my best smooth Danville Typing Service manner.

"Pure coincidence."

"Never! I can't believe it."

"True."

"You mean to say you'd no idea you'd see him here?"

"Nothing was further from my mind. I came to work on a new background for my next book."

"Oh, of course. You had a book published. I heard something about it from Ian. Well done. You've given up being a typist, then, I suppose? That was what you went off to do, wasn't it?"

The years had not improved Janet's manner. Always a little blunt, she now seemed to have acquired the kind of patronising dictatorial manner which I associated with minor bureaucrats. She had unusually brilliant blue-green eyes, and I met them steadily now as I replied.

"I manage a typing business still, but I'm thinking of easing myself out and giving all my time to writing eventually. And you?"

"Oh, I'm chief physiotherapist in the same clinic, but we've grown enormously." She stared at me. "I still find it hard to believe that you and Gareth arrived independently at this little hotel."

"A small world, isn't it?" I said smoothly, half smiling to myself as I used the same cliché with which Gareth had parried my surprise.

"A chance in a hundred. A bit off-putting, wasn't it? Meeting him unexpectedly like that."

"Why should it be? A lot has happened in the past four years. It seems a life-time ago, when I knew Gareth. Not relevant any more," I said, remembering Gareth's reply to that statement, but quite unrepentant as I smiled at Janet, who looked at me suspiciously. I was suddenly enjoying myself.

"And was Gareth pleased to see you? I doubt it. You gave the most awful sock to his pride, and he's not the forgiving type."

"We haven't seen a lot of each other, but he's been pleasant enough. What brings you here, Janet? Another coincidence?"

"No. I came over last Monday to spend a week with Ian. He happened to mention yesterday, just as I was thinking of going home, that Gareth had paid him a flying visit on his way for a month's holiday here. He'd been laid low by some bugs in Africa, and was taking convalescent leave, I gathered. It's over two years since I've seen him. In fact, I didn't know he was back from Africa. I couldn't go home without seeing him, knowing he was so near. He's one of our oldest friends, and I was a bit worried about this bug. So I adjusted my plans and came on here. If only Ian had mentioned it earlier in the week, I would have come before. As it is, I'll have to fly back tomorrow afternoon. Haven't seen Gareth yet. He's out, I expect. Is he well?"

"He seems to be very fit now. Been climbing a lot."

"That's good. Difficult to treat these bugs sometimes. We don't know enough about them."

She seemed genuinely concerned, and I felt more warmly disposed towards her.

"I'd say he's got the better of it, whatever it was."

"Did you know he'd been ill?"

"No. I don't know anything about Gareth's life since we split up. I had heard that he'd gone out to Africa on a job. That's all."

"Has he changed? Handsome old devil. Well, perhaps not handsome, but compelling in that Heathcliff sort of way."

"He hasn't changed much in appearance. And nor have you," I added, anxious to get off the subject of Gareth.

"You have," she said abruptly. "Out of all recognition. You

were such a raw child then. It's obviously done you a world of good, making your own way."

"I've enjoyed the experience."

"When do you go back?"

"I leave here next Thursday. I'm driving back. Aim to get home on Saturday."

"Home being?"

"I'm driving straight to Bray Hill to spend the week-end with my father and Aunt Ella before returning to my flat in London, and so back to work."

"How long have you been here?"

"Three weeks so far."

"The same time as Gareth?"

"Just about."

"Some people are lucky, having such long holidays."

"This is the first I've had for four years. And I've been doing some work here."

"Oh, writing." She obviously dismissed this as having no connection with work. "Odd for Gareth to take such a long break, being a partner in the firm and always so busy."

"I wouldn't know," I said gently, "but convalescence came into it, you said."

She looked at me sharply. I could see that she still nursed the suspicion that Gareth and I had plotted this.

"You were well out of that, Kate. Gareth might be a marvellous lover, but as a husband he'd be impossible. Look where he'd got you. His slave. It was pathetic."

"Old history now, Janet."

"Well, anyone can see how much better off you are without him. No plans in other directions?"

"Plenty," I said, wilfully obtuse, for I was getting irritated by her inquisitiveness.

"Matrimonial plans, I meant."

"Oh. No, I'm intent on becoming an established writer, and have no other plans."

"Very sensible, too. You're attractive, though, Kate. More now than you used to be, and there was always something about you. Beware the wolves."

"I'm well equipped now."

"Once bitten. You always were dead nuts on writing, weren't you? Didn't you have some sort of junior reporter's job on the local paper?"

"Yes. It wasn't bad training, either."

"You'd have done better in London."

"Perhaps." I remembered the struggle I'd had when the London job was open to me, torn between the wider experience it offered and the realisation that it would mean living in London, when Gareth at that time was living with his father in the next road to ours, and working at all sorts of odd hours. Gareth had pointed out how little time we should have together and was dead against it. I had turned the job down.

"Anyway, I'm glad it's all worked out so well for you," said Janet heartily. "I must read your book. Will the public library have it, do you think?"

"It's possible," I said demurely.

"Wonder what Gareth thought of Africa. Is he engaged or anything, do you know?"

"I have no idea."

"Safety in numbers, I guess. Well, I don't blame him. Plenty of willing victims, no doubt. If I were you I'd steer clear of him, though, Kate. He'd like to get his own back, and he could be a dangerous character. You hit him where it hurt. His masculine pride. The complete autocrat. No female ever did that to him before, I'll bet. He'd like to get you crawling again, just for the pleasure of telling you that opportunity doesn't come twice where he's concerned."

"He could be dangerous, yes. But not, I think, vindictive. However, you're mistaken in thinking there could be any life left in that old episode."

"Gareth doesn't forget."

"We've both moved on since then."

"Is he much changed, then?"

"In some ways, perhaps. But I really haven't seen a lot of him.

You must judge for yourself. Now it's nearly lunch time and I want to freshen up. You'll like this hotel, I think. Lucky they could take you at such short notice."

"Yes. They're full up again from Monday, though. Otherwise I might have been tempted to try to extend my leave."

"I'll see you later then." I hesitated. She was, after all, an old acquaintance. "If you'd like a drive round this afternoon, I'll be glad to show you the country. It's very beautiful."

"Oh, thanks. But I'll wait and see Gareth."

I had a feeling that she would wait a long time, and I felt sorry for her as I went up to my room. How blind I must have been, not to have realised that she was in love with him, even in the old days. Now her obsession was only too plain, and the years had not diminished it. Her brother's oldest friend. She had probably been in love with him before I met him. And her own jealousy had coloured the report she had given me about him, had made her seem so concerned for me, when in reality I was the destroyer of her hopes. And I had only seen her, innocently, as the candid friend. How much had she influenced me? Not a great deal, I thought, in making the final decision, for the reasons for that had been growing within me for months past. But she had added bitter gall to the unhappiness that was already there, and had made that last row an uglier one than it need have been. It was Gareth, perhaps, who had suffered most from her tongue, because he had blown up and said things which otherwise would not have occurred to him, and my decision was thus made final.

I was standing by the window of my room looking down at the coutryard, but seeing only that last scene. Gareth's white, furious face, outraged that I should question his loyalty and honesty. Myself, frightened, angry, shattered, but clinging desperately to the resolve in my mind to escape from this tyranny of love to a freedom where I could find myself again. It had been a cataclysmic experience. I had never known or met before such violence of feeling. And from the dust and ruins afterwards, I'd had to start again.

It was a long time since that cataclysm had last risen to re-enact itself in my mind, for I had succeeded in locking it away after the first year alone. I thought I had buried it for ever. Now it came back to mock me.

That afternoon, I went out with my notebook in my pocket, found a sunny perch on the hillside behind the hotel and did some plotting, forcing my mind to concentrate on the spider's web of my plot, so that the sun had gone and I felt chilly when I came out of my imaginary world to find that it was nearly half past six and once more I had forgotten all about tea.

I met Janet hanging about the drive to the hotel when I got back. She looked despondent and bored, but put on a brisk, humorous air as she said:

"I'm still waiting for his lordship. You haven't seen him anywhere, I suppose?"

"Not a glimpse. I think the weather's on the change."

"Well, I hope he turns up soon. I've only got until tomorrow afternoon."

I could not persuade her to come down to the village with me after dinner, and when I got back about ten o'clock, she was still sitting in the lounge, thumbing over some magazines with a very dejected air. I joined her.

"I asked the waiter about Gareth," she said. "He said he'd telephoned to say he'd not be in to dinner. What do you suppose he's up to?"

"There's plenty of scope for exploration round here, and he always was a restless type."

"Guess I'm unlucky. Wish I'd telephoned to let him know I was coming, but it all had to be fixed in such a rush, and I thought I'd surprise him," she added with an awkward little laugh.

I didn't tell her that he knew she was here. I asked for a pot of tea, and chatted away about the Grossglockner, but Janet hardly appeared to be listening and the atmosphere of constraint gripped me, too, in the end, and I fell silent, annoyed with Gareth for leaving me to provide the sops for his absence. You shouldn't be so soft, Kate, I could hear him say.

And then I jumped as a hand touched my shoulder and Gareth stood in front of us.

"Well, girls," he said, "can I join the tea party? This is unexpected, Janet."

"Gareth!" she exclaimed, her face split with a smile. "How good to see you after all this time! When Ian told me you were here, I simply had to come and see you. I've been staying with Ian for a week. He didn't tell me you were here until yesterday."

Gareth's face had assumed a poker quality which I knew spelt danger. His voice and manner were excessively formal in response to this effusion.

"I hope you'll like Mölden. Are you staying long?"

"Unfortunately, I have to go back tomorrow afternoon. But I'll be able to see something of you now that you're back in London. You're looking better than I expected. Ian said you'd been laid low with a bug and were looking pretty seedy when he saw you."

"The mountains have taken care of that. Can I get you girls a nightcap? Kate?"

I refused as I was still on tea, but Janet asked for a whisky and soda, and Gareth went off to the little cocktail bar adjoining the dining-room. Janet said nothing while he was gone, watching the door for his return, and I was dumb, too, feeling a tension in the air which I did not know how to relieve. When he returned with two glasses of whisky on a tray, he pulled up a capacious armchair opposite us, and leaned back, glass in hand, surveying the pair of us through narrowed eyes.

"Well, I suppose you two have been getting up to date," he said blandly.

"Extraordinary, Kate being here!" exclaimed Janet. "Pure coincidence, she says."

If he says it's a small world again, I thought, I'll scream. But he merely gave Janet a polite smile and said:

"A happy coincidence indeed."

"What have you been doing with yourself? Three weeks is a long time in one place."

"Climbing. Motoring. No shortage of things to do. Even Kate's found it hard to work here with so many tempting distractions."

There was a wicked gleam in his eyes as they met mine, and I wanted to throw something at him. Before I could say anything, Janet broke in:

"Tell me about Africa, Gareth. Disappearing like that into the blue, and never a card."

"Ian and I never have been good correspondents. Africa was very steamy, but it's far too large a subject to be discussed at this time of night."

"Well, I want to hear all about it tomorrow. Where are you staying in London, by the way? Ian said you didn't leave him your address. Somewhere in Kensington, he thought."

"It's only a temporary address. I haven't had time to make any permanent plans yet. You're still in the same job?"

"Yes. A bit higher up the ladder, though. I hope you'll not be disappearing again to some distant country, Gareth. There are plenty of engineering jobs to be done at home, after all."

"Wherever duty calls," he said, his eyes contemplating my legs, so that I pulled at my rather short skirt, a gesture which I regretted when I saw his lips twitch.

He stone-walled Janet's questions with unswerving politeness, cool as a cucumber, and I was wriggling my toes inside my shoes with the tension of it. I was about to make my excuses and leave them alone, which was what Janet so patently desired, since she had ignored me completely after Gareth's arrival, when he forestalled me.

"If you'll both excuse me. I'm making an early start tomorrow."

"A start where?" I demanded.

"A reconnaissance tour in the car, to decide which mountain it shall be for my last climb. Time's running out. I probably shan't see you again, Janet, so I'll say good-bye. I hope you'll have a good journey home."

"But Gareth, I've only got tomorrow morning here, and I came specially to see you," cried Janet, all pretences swept aside.

"That was rash of you, my dear. I'm sorry. But you'll have Kate to keep you company. Good-night."

He gave us an affable salute and went off with the tray and two empty glasses. We were alone in the lounge and I had to sit and listen to Janet's tirade.

"Arrogant brute! Who does he think he is? To treat an old friend like that! We've known Gareth since he was at school. I can't say Africa's improved him. He always was stony-hearted, but this takes the prize . . ."

It went on and on, and there was nothing I could do to stop it. I felt sorry for her. Gareth had been politely brutal. I should have felt skinned in her place, but she should never have put herself in that position. Gareth was the last person in the world to have his hand forced.

Franz came in, looked startled at what he heard before Janet clamped her lips together in a hard line, and in the silence that ensued he hastily gathered the tea-things together and scuttled out.

"Well, let's make the best of it and enjoy a morning out tomorrow," I said.

"No thank you. I know when I'm not wanted," declared Janet, red-faced. "Anyway, I came to see Gareth. Since he's going to be out all day, I shall go to Innsbruck in the morning and spend the rest of my time there."

I ignored her rudeness, but it was not, as I had thought, her bitter disappointment and her flayed feelings after Gareth's cruel handling that made her ignore my sensibilities, for she now turned a look of vindictive anger on me and said:

"Don't think I'm taken in by your pretence that it was chance, your being here at the same time as Gareth. You're up to something. I can tell that from the way you look at him. Don't tell me you didn't come here after him."

"If I had, that would make two of us, wouldn't it?" I said, my anger spurting.

"You don't deny it, then?"

"I certainly do. I came here with a friend, who stayed with me for the first week, and my sole aim and object was to get some work done on a new book. I had no idea Gareth would be here. Believe it or not, as you please."

"I suppose you thought he'd be impressed with your achievements. The clever little writer. Well, I can tell you this. Gareth

Ferrion will have only one idea in his head where you're concerned: to get his own back. It would amuse him to make you come crawling again, as you used to, just for the pleasure of punishing you before showing you the door. There's a dangerous streak in Gareth. I'm warning you."

"Do you suppose I don't know him as well as you?"

"Know him? You only worshipped him with a sickly calf love. You were pathetic. I've known him and loved him and hated him ever since he and Ian were at school together. I've never been able to get him out of my system, more fool me. But he'll not have you, either. I can tell you that."

But it seemed to me that Janet had told me quite enough for one evening. I said good-night and left her, but I was too angry and restless to go to bed, and I fetched a coat, changed my shoes, and slipped out. It was a clear night, but there was a cold nip in the air and nobody was lingering in the courtyard. I turned up the hill, glad of the cool air against my burning cheeks. The stream tumbled palely beside me and the distant peaks, cold and remote, seemed to mock the follies of human passions. I felt sorry for Janet, now that my anger was cooling. What foolish vulnerable creatures women were, I thought, with their capacity for love. Janet had been in the grip of this obsession for Gareth from her adolescent days, and she was in her late twenties now. I knew Gareth well enough to be sure that he had never encouraged her, but it was obviously impossible for her to accept the hopelessness of her situation, to put it behind her. I thought about her suggestion that Gareth might be out for revenge. There was a passionate streak of pride in him. It was not impossible, but there was nothing small about Gareth. I thought it very unlikely that he was plotting for revenge like a Borgia.

I was standing on the bank watching the water flow by when he joined me, silently, so that I jumped.

"I had to make sure it wasn't Janet," he said, putting a steadying hand on my shoulder.

"You were cruel."

"I had to be. Nothing less would suffice."

"Surely you needn't have been quite so heartless."

"You don't understand the position, Kate. You must allow me to know best in this case."

"I do understand it. More than I did, anyway. Janet was in no mood to hide her feelings after you'd gone. I got the full force of it."

"I'm sorry. It's been an embarrassment for more years than I can remember. Spoilt my friendship with Ian, in a way. I welcomed the chance to get in touch with him here, knowing Janet was in London. There are no kind ways of telling a person that you can't return their feelings, Kate. And with a person as tough in the hide as Janet, there aren't even any polite ways."

"I suppose not. I got the rough edge of her tongue, though, not you."

"If I say I'm glad, it's because I feared that you and she would be ganging up. I guessed she'd jump at the chance of feeding the old trouble between us."

"I told her that the past was dead. All of it."

"Did she believe you?"

"Not altogether. The coincidence of our both being here takes some swallowing, after all."

"Quite."

"Why *did* you come here, Gareth? Was it that hundredth chance or did you know I'd be here?"

"I came for a holiday. And if you think I came for anything else, perhaps I'll be able to enlighten you when we have that talk you're going to ask me for. Remember?"

I remembered that night in the car when he had kissed me. And afterwards the hard edge to his voice. "When you're ready to talk, let me know. You shall ask for that unfinished business to be completed, not I?" The words had been branded in my mind. Now they seemed to take on a more sinister threat in the light of Janet's warning. Was I wrong in thinking him incapable of such cruelty? It would amuse him to make you come crawling again, Janet had said. To punish you for the injury to his pride. I shivered, unable to reject it as I had a few minutes ago.

"You're so certain that I'm going to ask you?" I said.

He took me in his arms, and must have felt my shivering. Then he tilted my face up with firm fingers.

"I think you will, Kate," he said quietly. "I think you will, even though Janet has no doubt been at work again with her little hatchet."

"I'm not so easily influenced now as I was once. I have a mind of my own."

"Then you certainly will ask for that debate, because you're a fair-minded person and you must know that I've a right to have the opportunity to answer that long letter you wrote me."

"That was four years ago. I was a different person then. It's finished," I said recklessly.

"When I see indifference on your face, when I touch you and you're unmoved, I'll accept that. You're lying, Kate. You know, and I know, that it's unfinished business between us. Why are you afraid to talk about it? You've just said you have a mind of your own now. Use it, then, and convince me, and stop running away from the issue. What are you frightened of?"

"What do you expect to gain from raking over those old ashes?" I parried. "Do you want to make me say that I was wrong, that I'm sorry, so that you can punish me as you punished Janet tonight? That's it, isn't it?"

The words slipped from me almost in spite of myself. Janet's description of me, "pathetic", was still stinging. He released me at once, and his voice held an angry bitterness I had never heard before.

"So that's what you think of me! That for four years I've been harbouring a grudge against you. That all our broken engagement meant to me was a dent in my vanity and that now, like some mean little schoolboy, I'm ready with my pea-shooter to get my own back. God, what age do you think I am, Kate? What sort of a man do you think I am?"

"I . . . I never meant . . ." I stumbled.

"Don't bother to spare my feelings," he said cuttingly. "Since you think that of me, you're very sensible to want to steer clear of me. There's no more to be said."

He had gone before I could say another word, leaving me

trembling and lacerated. Wretchedly, I walked back to the hotel, oppressed by Janet's words and a self-flaying anger with myself for getting caught up in this emotional tangle with Gareth. I had learnt nothing. Why on earth had I been so foolish as to think I could stay under the same roof as Gareth Ferrion and not be involved again in the web I'd struggled from with such pain and effort four years before? In a nightmarish way, the circumstances of this evening had been a repetition of what had happened before. The talk with Janet, the accusation of what Gareth would consider dishonourable conduct, and his furious reaction. Only this time he had not blown up but had left me, coldly, decisively. And the ultimate irony was that although what I had said this time had had the desired effect of sending him away, I was miserably unhappy about the whole business. I should never have stayed to get involved; I might have known that my new found confidence was still not enough to stand out against the power Gareth had over me; I should have run away, have returned with John at the end of that first week.

Over and over in my mind that night the arguments plagued me, the arguments I thought I'd settled once and for all. Gareth had the pride of Lucifer. This time, I felt he really meant that there was no more to be said. There you are, then. You've got what you want. But I had won with an unfair blow. Gareth was not a petty man, whatever else he was. I had allowed Janet's cruel words to me to flay my pride, and I in turn had flayed his. Angrily, I shook up my pillow, tried to shut my mind to the confusion of my thoughts, and in the end, when dawn was breaking, fell into a sleep of exhaustion.

13

Mutual Aid

I WAS LATER than usual down to breakfast the next morning, and the dining-room was empty except for Janet.

"You look a sick dog this morning," she said, coming over to my table. She had finished her breakfast and had been lingering over a paper.

"Bit of a headache," I said shortly, wishing she would go away.

"I got up early, hoping to catch Gareth, but he'd gone. Beats me why people have to work so hard on holiday. You'll need to be spry to put salt on his tail, Kate."

"You do have a one-track mind," I said, buttering some toast, finding her staring eyes and bossy nurse-knows-best attitude hard to take just then.

"Don't you?" she asked with a malicious little smile.

"Yes. My book. I'm in the middle of working out a complicated plot. Excuse me if I don't seem chatty."

"Offended by what I said last night, I suppose. It was all true, you know. Only trying to save you coming another cropper."

"That's kind of you, but I'm well able to take care of myself. You'll find Innsbruck an interesting town, and the public gardens are delightful. Have you arranged transport?"

"Yes. I'm just going to pack. I must say friend Gareth has put me to a lot of needless expense."

I said nothing. If she chose to chase a man who had given her no encouragement, it was her funeral. And then something in her eyes made me sorry for her again. The tyranny of love. Driven by an obsession, courting humiliation and snubs, she seemed a pitiful soul. But again, as so often in the past, she drove out sympathy by her utter lack of sensibility.

"He's put you to even more expense, I guess. Nice to think one isn't the only fool."

"I came here to get new material for my next book."

"Knowing Gareth was going to be here? Who are you kidding?" said Janet.

I sacrificed my second cup of coffee and stood up.

"If you'll excuse me, I've work to do. Good-bye. And a safe journey."

I went back to my room, my head thudding, and stood by the window pressing my hands to my temples. I thought of my expectations of a peaceful, quiet holiday, of my happy mood when I set out. I thought of John, of the Danville Typing Service, my writing; the busy, satisfying life I had left behind. How had I managed to get into this ugly tangle? How was I going to get back?

I waited until I saw Janet leave before emerging from my room, for I had had as much of her as I could take. Then I went for a walk through the wood between the hotel and the village, trying to sort myself out. When I came out of the wood on to the road which led back to the hotel, I saw Monsieur Corbeil ahead, walking very slowly. Something in his laboured step made me run to catch up with him. He turned a grey face to me.

"You're ill. Can I help?"

"It is nothing. I have just taken one of my little pills. It will pass."

"Rest here a minute." I took his arm and helped him to a low stone wall.

To my relief, after a short rest he seemed to have recovered, and gave me a little smile.

"I frightened you, chérie. No need to worry. I am used to these little spells. I walked up a hill back there. I should have known better. Don't let me detain you. I assure you that I'm quite all right now."

"I was thinking of a nice peaceful pot of coffee in the courtyard. Will that suit you?"

"Indeed, I had the same thing in mind."

He seemed glad of the arm I offered him and we walked slowly back to the hotel. I kept quiet, and installed him at my favourite table by the fountain before going to order coffee from Franz. We were alone in the courtyard. It was quiet and sunny and peaceful there.

"You, too, look a little pale today," said my companion, surveying me with his shrewd dark eyes.

"I slept badly last night. But you? Shouldn't you see a doctor?"

"My doctor has said and done all that is necessary, chérie. There is nothing to worry about."

I realised, with a shock, what the expression in his eyes meant. I hesitated, then I said:

"You're so calm. So untroubled. Ought you to be travelling unaccompanied?"

"There are times when solitude is desirable. This pilgrimage I am making to all the places I have loved is best savoured alone. I have plenty of memories to keep me company, and an opportunity for contemplation. We lead such busy lives that we leave ourselves no time for contemplation, and are the worse for it."

"I hope they're happy memories and that contemplation doesn't leave any bitter taste."

"Well, life's an odd mixture. We need the bitter as well as the sweet, perhaps. We learn from the hurts. After all, it is only pain that teaches us courage, that helps us to gain a little insight and self-knowledge, and from that we gain strength. You know what Schopenhauer said? 'The fruit of life is experience not happiness, and its fruition to accustom ourselves, and to be content, to exchange hope for insight.'"

"My father is fond of quoting him. I've always thought him a depressing man."

"For the young, perhaps. I have reached the age of acceptance, but you are still at the age of striving and hope. And you have not solved your problems?" he added with a little smile.

"How trivial they must seem to you!"

"Affairs of the heart trivial? It is my misfortune if they seem so. And you are troubled, I can see. The young man has not reassured you?"

"It's in myself, the conflict. He's like a magnet pulling me one way while my mind tells me that if I once yield, I'm lost. That our marriage would be either a disaster, or, for me, a prison. No, not a prison. That's too bleak a suggestion. There would be comfort and some happiness and enjoyment, as well as domination."

"He would be your falconer and you the captive bird on his wrist, loved and cherished, with a line to limit your flight?"

"Very apt," I said, smiling. "We're unsuited. Gareth's a splendid person in so many ways; he'd make some gentle, submissive girl wonderfully happy. But he and I would always be scrapping unless I submitted, and we'd hurt each other terribly. I couldn't bear that. We've done enough damage to each other as it is."

"Before, when you were engaged. You ... what do you say ... scrapped?"

"No. I tried, at the end, but he could always take me in his arms and drown my arguments. I'm such a weak, flabby character where Gareth's concerned."

"No, chérie. That I will not have. Too much in love, perhaps."

"It's kind of you to make excuses, but the fact is that Gareth's will was always too strong for me. Do you know, at the end, I couldn't make any decisions for myself? I always thought, what will Gareth want to do? Will Gareth like that? My little flags of independence that tried to flutter at the end were pulled down so easily with a smile and a kiss. And in the end, when you're treated as though you've no mind of your own, when it's taken for granted that you're tractable, there whenever you're wanted, content to wait when you're not, you somehow grow like that. It's a frightening experience; to feel yourself dissolving into a shapeless nonentity."

There was a pause during which Monsieur Corbeil sipped his coffee thoughtfully. Then he said slowly:

"Do you not think it possible that it was lack of confidence in yourself that was a little to blame, and that now you are older and have gained confidence in yourself, have achieved independence, it would not be the same? Are you not making the mistake of seeing it all too much in terms of the past?"

"Gareth is the same dominating character."

"No man but a saint, chérie, would not take advantage of a girl who adored him to impose his mastery. English men particularly, I feel, have inherited a tradition of treating women as their servants. For all the talk of equality of the sexes, in your country it is far from being accepted. But he is intelligent, that young man. Could you not convince him?"

"I haven't tried. As I said, once I give an inch, I'm lost."

"I think you underrate your newly achieved confidence. You must either have faith in it and make the attempt to heal the differences, or put an ocean between you and that young man. It is difficult to be detached when physical attraction is playing its undermining tricks, but you must make the effort, dig down deeply into your mind and heart to find the truth and then take your courage in both hands and act on it, and not look back."

"I'll try. Things can't go on like this. It's a strain on both of us. But Gareth is a formidable opponent. The pressure's relentless," I added, and my voice wobbled.

Monsieur Corbeil put a hand on my arm.

"Courage, Kate. You can be a little formidable yourself, if you must. Now I will have a short rest before lunch. Thank you for your help this morning. There is such warm sympathy in those brown eyes; no wonder your falconer still aims to recapture his falcon," he concluded with a little chuckle as he left me.

It sounded so easy. Search your mind and heart. But I'd been searching mine for weeks past, and no clear answer had emerged. I wished, in that moment of tiredness, that something would force my hand. But, whatever I decided, I was going to take back what I'd said to Gareth the previous night. He had not deserved that, and I was ashamed of myself for allowing the stings which Janet had inflicted to goad me into that injustice.

I was unable to work that afternoon, and took myself off for a stiff climb up a foothill on the opposite side of the valley from the hotel. The sky was overcast, and the cooler air was welcome for the effort entailed. I sat down and had a rest on the top, trying to identify the mountain peaks now visible to me in the distance. I wondered which mountain Gareth would choose on his reconnaissance that day, and when he would be back. Early this evening probably, since he knew that Janet was catching the afternoon plane from Innsbruck.

I was half-way down the hill again when I came out on to a bluff which looked straight down to the road below, and there at a bend I saw a knot of people, a lorry and a wrecked car, and as I watched, a stretcher was carried from behind the car to a waiting ambulance. It was a grey car, and looked enough like a Mercedes to send me racing down the hair-pin bends of the hill, feeling sick with dread. The face of the victim on the stretcher had been covered by the blanket. Gareth had always driven too fast, I thought. Today, bitter and angry after my wounding remarks the previous night, he might well have been in no mood for caution. Please God, I prayed, please God, not Gareth.

The hair-pin bends seemed interminable. I heard the lorry drive off, and as I slithered round the last bend, I saw the ambulance disappearing in the opposite direction. The road was empty when I reached it, and I raced along to the wrecked car, half on its side, its bonnet crushed against the stone wall into which it had run. It was a Mercedes. I could see from the tangle that had once been the front of the car that the impact must have killed the driver instantly. The number plate was obliterated against the wall. I went round to the back with my legs suddenly threatening to give way under me. The car had slewed round against a tree and I could not see the rear number plate either. Only a GB plate told me that it was British. I tried to see into the wreckage, but it was a shambles of broken glass, twisted metal, scattered remnants that told me nothing of the identity of the owner.

I leaned against the tree. It was uncannily silent now in the narrow, twisting road. Then I was running like a stag along the short distance to the hotel track. Fear lent me a speed I would never otherwise have attained, and I passed Monsieur Corbeil like a streak of lightning as I made for the car park. If it's not there, I thought, he may still be all right. Still be out. But, please God, let it be there. My hair was wet with perspiration and my heart was pounding so painfully that I was gasping and my eyes seemed bleary, but not too bleary to see Gareth's car standing there, gleaming and unscathed. I sank down beside it, utterly spent, and cried over the boot.

"Chérie. What is it? What has happened?"

Monsieur Corbeil's drawn, concerned face brought me back to the realisation that he had hurried after me and was in no state of health to do so. I was still gulping for air.

"N . . . nothing. It's all right. I saw a car smashed up. It looked like Gareth's." I pulled myself up, half gasping, and hung over the car, recovering myself.

Monsieur Corbeil waited a minute or two, and then took my arm, saying with a little smile:

"Now it is my turn to come to your rescue with a pot of tea. Take it easily. You have had a shock."

And indeed, although the nightmare receded while I sipped my tea in the quiet courtyard with Monsieur Corbeil, I still felt shaky and appalled. It was not Gareth, thank God, but somebody, somewhere, had to face the grief. So brutal, so sudden.

"Life seems so uncertain. So dangerous," I said, my lips trembling. "You make plans, you love, and it can all be wiped out in a minute."

"The razor's edge. Try to put it out of your mind, Kate. You can do nothing about it. I think you should go and lie down and take some aspirin."

"Yes, I will. You've been so kind."

"This is our day for mutual aid. You feel things too deeply. That is a disadvantage in this world of ours. You may not think you need protection, but you do. You are not tough, like the glamorous Mrs Chagford," he added with his odd, tolerant little smile.

"You may be right. It was kind but unwise of you to hurry after me like that."

"And you, fleeing like a stricken deer from the hounds of hell?"

"Thank you for your kindness. If I lie down now, whatever's thumping in my head like a hammer may stop."

I smiled at him and turned to go.

"Chérie," he said, and I looked back. "You are fighting something too strong for you."

"Could be."

The quiet peace of my room welcomed me. I closed the shutters, took two aspirins, and let the cool smoothness of the pillow take my aching head.

14

Landmark

DETAILS OF THE accident had filtered through to the hotel when I went into the little cocktail lounge that evening. The victim, an elderly man, travelling on business ... a dangerous speed ... the lorry leaving little room on the bend. I did not want to discuss it and took my glass of sherry to the quiet corner where Monsieur Corbeil was sitting alone, as usual.

He gave me an enquiring look as he greeted me.

"Better? Yes, I can see."

"Much better, thanks. That book you recommended to me the other day. I've lost the piece of paper I wrote on and I've forgotten the author's name."

I jotted it down again, and we chatted about books and authors. Gareth came in, gave me a chilly "Good-evening", and joined a group by the bar, ordering a whisky and soda. He looked as inviting as an east wind. Nevertheless, the east wind had to be faced, and I laid my hand on his arm as several of us were making our way to the dining-room.

"Can you spare me a few moments after dinner, Gareth? There's something I want to say to you. In the courtyard?"

"Very well," he said with cold formality.

It had turned humid and close that evening, and the sky was grey. I carried my coffee to Gareth's table in the courtyard, and came straight to the point.

"I want to apologise for what I said last night, Gareth. In my heart, I knew it wasn't true."

"Then why did you say it?"

"Janet, talking of the past, said I was pathetic, the way I used to crawl to you. That nothing would please you more than to have me doing it again so that you could get your own back. I didn't believe what she said about you, but my pride was hurt, the more so because what she said about me, anyway, was true. And I took it out of you, and that was unforgivable. I'm truly sorry."

"All right," he said, his eyes searching mine. "We'll forget it. But let's fight this out with our own weapons, Kate. Not the dirty ones other people put in our hands."

"Last night is something I'd like to blot out. You were cruel to Janet and she took it out of me. And I allowed her cruelty to me to bounce off on you. But your cruelty was necessary, and mine wasn't. I'm not proud of myself."

"Janet always has been a dispenser of trouble. She's an unhappy, frustrated woman, and makes sure other people pay for it. I'm glad she's gone."

"I intended to catch you before you left this morning, but I overslept."

"You look a bit washed out. Are you all right?"

"Yes, quite all right."

"You asked me last night, among other things, what I expected to gain from raking over the old ashes. It's time you knew. I should have thought it was obvious. I agree that we've moved on, and that these four years between have made a big difference. But I still believe that basically you and I belong. If we're to come together again, though, we've got to build on new foundations. We can't do that without examining the old to understand what went wrong. You've been running away from that as though I were the devil tempting you, but in all fairness, surely I deserve the chance you never gave me before of answering that letter, even if on Thursday we go our separate ways and never see each other again. I'm not going to ask you again. I told you that there comes a time to stop asking. I won't press you any more. It must be your decision now. Just think over what I've said."

"Yes, I will."

Silence fell between us for a few minutes. I looked at his profile; he was studying the well-head with a brooding expression. A passionate, complex character, with a steely will, great ability, an authority so natural to him that he wasn't even aware of it, a devilish temper, a poetic sensibility, a brutal ruthlessness, and an uncompromising mind. It all added up to a very difficult proposition. And a wily campaigner. He had sensed a difference in me. Knew I had stopped running. And had relaxed the pressure instantly, well aware of the old wrestlers' trick of releasing the opponent suddenly so that he was unbalanced. I knew him better now than I had done before, when I was young and blinded by first love. I was older, with more experience of the world, and this holiday had taught me more of the man that was Gareth Ferrion. His dealings with others—Mrs Chagford, Roger and Ann, Miss Courtland—as well as with me, had helped me to see him in the round. And one result of this was that I had lost the fear of him that had lurked behind my early infatuation and my first weeks here. I wasn't afraid any more.

"Which mountain have you decided to tackle tomorrow?" I asked.

"The Venhorn."

"Will you be starting early?"

"Not specially. I shall sleep at the mountain hut tomorrow night and go for the peak on Tuesday morning. Too big a job for one day."

"I thought of exploring the lower slopes myself tomorrow. Ann and I found some wild cyclamen there. I shall drive to the foot of the valley where the path starts. Would it be any help to give you a lift there and save the slogging along the road?"

"Thanks. It would. Nine-ish. Would that be too early for you?"

"No. I'll be ready."

"The weather forecast's not all that good, but Franz thinks it'll be all right on this side of the mountain. I should come prepared for rain if you intend to make a day of it."

"I will."

"How's the book going?"

"Not too well. That's why I want to have the day out tomorrow. That mountain offers a good setting for one episode in my plot. I want to study it in more detail."

"The proprietor's promised to lend me a map and give me a few tips about the final stretch to the peak, so if you'll excuse me, I'll go and find him. I'll see you in the morning."

"Right."

He left me to my thoughts. I had come out of the panicky confusion of the past weeks, and found my mind clear and working well. The accident that afternoon, when I had thought Gareth was dead, had had a cathartic effect, and for the first time since that initial encounter with him here I felt able to do what Monsieur Corbeil had recommended, to dig down deeply into my mind and my heart for the truth and then to act on it. I went back over the past with a detachment which I had been unable to attain before, starting from that very first meeting with Gareth when I was on what I had expected to be a routine job of reporting for my local paper a public enquiry into a planning application for building on an open space on the outskirts of Bray Hill. Gareth had spoken against it with a passion and eloquence which had transformed the meeting, galvanising it to life. And for me, nothing had ever been the same again. I remembered that when I had approached him afterwards to check his name for my report, my hand had been shaking so much that I could hardly write while his dark eyes had watched me, amused. He had telephoned me the next day. In a month, we were engaged.

And so it had started, the year's delirium, during which I had passed from rapture, through enslavement and pitiful little efforts to assert my individuality, to the final stage of humiliation when I knew I had become a weak puppet, treated by Gareth as a toy to be petted when he was in the mood, or put aside when other demands on his time were more important. And then those two last week-ends. I went over them again in my mind, seeing them almost as plays, myself a spectator.

First the Easter week-end when I had forfeited my dearest wish to go to Greece with my father. There had never been much money available for travel in my family, and this trip was occasioned by a small and unexpected legacy which had come to my father. But Gareth had proposed a visit to Wales for the holiday week-end, and, of course, there was no doubt where my choice rested, although it was a wrench to forgo the twelve days in

Greece. Aunt Ella had gone with my father instead, and I had the house to myself. Gareth had telephoned on the Thursday evening, from Paddington. Some serious trouble had arisen on a motorway construction for which his firm were the consulting engineers, and there was to be an on the spot conference immediately. He was on his way then, and it looked as though he would be away the whole week-end. He had cancelled our booking at the Welsh farmhouse. He expressed his regret at spoiling my week-end, but in a voice which suggested that his mind was on the problems awaiting him. I had spent the week-end alone, weeding the garden, reading, sick with disappointment.

To make up for this, Gareth promised that we would go to Wales the following week-end. He could have the Friday off to make up for working over Easter, and if I could get the same concession, we would drive to Wales on Friday morning, return on Sunday evening. He would telephone the farmhouse, whose owners he knew very well. Then on Thursday evening, he came round with an entirely different scheme. Ian and Janet had asked us to join them for a week-end at a climbing hotel in the Lake District. It was Ian's last week-end before taking up an appointment in Germany. Gareth had agreed to go. I had protested, for I had never felt at home with the Rentons, but Gareth had, as usual in such circumstances, taken me in his arms and sent my protests to roost.

It had been a tight squeeze in Gareth's car for the four of us, plus the men's climbing gear, which should have warned me. There were several climbers at the hotel, and the evening was spent in climbing talk, to which I had nothing to contribute. Two of the climbers were making an ambitious sortie the next day, taking in two peaks, and they invited Gareth and Ian to join them. Janet and I were not consulted. The party set off early the next morning. My pleas to Gareth to be allowed to go at least part of the way with them met with amused refusal. The idea of taking a novice was absurd. Janet and I misunderstood the programme, or else had been deliberately kept in the dark, for we expected them back that evening, and it was the proprietor who told us that they were spending the night in a mountain hostel and would not be back until Sunday midday. I was left with a sulky, resentful Janet for company, and it was during Sunday morning, when we were both angrily complaining about the men's behaviour, that Janet informed me that whatever I might have been told about the previous week-end's disappointment, which I had been describing to her, she had seen Gareth taking an attractive young woman into Scott's restaurant in London on the night of Easter Monday.

The climbers arrived back just in time for lunch, jubilant, full of their expedition. The journey back to London was painful in the extreme, with Janet not hiding her resentment, while I tried to mask my anger beneath a too polite façade for the benefit of Ian and Janet, saving it all up until Gareth and I were alone and he was not driving. We dropped Janet and Ian off at their home in Wimbledon and continued on our way to Bray Hill. I could remember as plainly as if it had been yesterday the silence in the car for that last hour's drive to Surrey. I would not distract Gareth while he was driving, and for the life of me I could find not one polite or trivial word to say. It was like sitting listening to the tick of the clock before the time bomb went off. I rounded on him in the hall. The house was empty still, for my father and Aunt Ella were not due back from Greece until the next day. And then the bomb exploded. And in a way, I thought, the reverberations had never quite stopped.

I found myself looking back at it now for the first time with calmness instead of distress, and realised that I had passed a landmark. I could see its causes and its inevitability, and although Janet's harsh reminder had bruised me again, I was comforted by the knowledge that confidence in myself and respect for myself were now part of me and not to be washed away by the resuscitation of the past. And that knowledge made all the difference. All the difference in the world.

I stayed there alone in the courtyard until it was dark and the lanterns created their own attractive landscape of light and shadow over the courtyard, lighting up some of the geraniums and marguerites in the window-boxes, leaving others in shadow so that only the marguerites glimmered like pale ghosts. There was no movement from the mountain ash tree. Only the fountain broke the stillness with its dancing drops and gentle music.

That night, thankful for the blessed return of detachment and confidence, of a mind I felt I could trust again, I slept peacefully and woke to a sunny morning and the realisation that I should have to hurry to keep my appointment with Gareth.

15

Climbing

I DROVE CAREFULLY, conscious of the critical eye of my passenger beside me. His knapsack, ice axe and coil of rope were stowed on the back seat. Trimly clad in navy blue ski pants, a thin light blue wool sweater with a polo neck and a navy windcheater, he managed to look elegant even in climbing gear. He evidently liked to travel light compared with the climbers I had seen staggering under great rucksacks from which various articles of hardware dangled. His equipment, his appearance and his manner that morning were all streamlined for a serious job of work.

I parked the car off the road at the foot of what was not so much a valley as a gully, which reared up starkly. It looked as though it might have been carved out by a glacier in the distant past, its bare scree base contained by dark cliffs of rock, the whole devoid of vegetation and singularly uninviting. Hard to believe that by taking a track up through woods nearby, one came out on to an alp where the grass was emerald green, wild flowers were abundant and ferns grew near a tumbling stream.

Gareth's path was mine for the first hour through the woods to the alp, and we sat down by the wooden bridge across the stream for a breather before he went on his way. He accepted one of my apples.

"Why do you do it? Climb the peaks, I mean? So arduous, sometimes dangerous, when beauty is all around you on these lower slopes where there's life and vegetation. Above the snow line, the world's dead," I said, looking at the sparkle of a dewdrop in the centre of a pale blue cup-shaped flower.

"Well, for all sorts of reasons, I guess," he said, taking a reflective bite out of his apple. "This time, rather different ones from the past."

"Such as?" I prompted.

"First, there's the challenge. The adventure. Especially when you're young. That aspect is fading for me a bit now. Then there's the solitude and beauty of the mountain heights, more truly away from it all than anywhere else I can think of. And the moments of glory which now and again reward you for your efforts. Perhaps the dawn breaking over the peak above you, or the lights of a village below when you come down at the end of a successful climb. When life for a brief moment is lived at a different level. You can get the same feeling from great music, from a painting, from less austere country, I know. There aren't so many moments of glory, though, that I'm not prepared to seek them wherever they may be found."

"I understand. I seek for them in less harsh spheres than the high mountains, though. Above the snow line I find them forbidding, dwarfing."

"Few women have the physique for them, anyway. There are less exalted reasons why I've taken up climbing again this holiday after a gap of some years, though. I wanted to test out my fitness. Harden up again after the soft effect of the tropics. Mountains are good places, too, I find, for thinking out one's problems, and for working off frustration by the hard physical effort they call for."

I didn't ask further about the frustration, but said, thinking that he had been alluding to his work:

"Do you have so many problems, then?"

"And *you* ask me that!" he said, lifting his eyes to heaven.

I skirted that, too, and eyed his equipment on the grass beside him.

"A rope, on your own?"

"M'm. Always handy. Especially for getting down awkward places quickly. Besides, I might team up with another climber at the hut."

"Gareth, isn't it dangerous, on your own?"

"Not this peak. I rather like to be a loner, anyway."

"What have you got in that knapsack? It looks little enough

compared with the climbers' rucksacks I've been seeing around."

"Some food, in case there isn't any at the hut or I don't reach it at the right time. A spare sweater and socks and a groundsheet in case I sleep out, a torch and some thin waterproof trousers to pull on over these if we get the rain Franz has prophesied. If the weather turns really sour, though, I shall come back."

"All that in such a small pack?" I asked, incredulously.

"I've got it to a fine art," he said, smiling. "Don't like going round like a packhorse. As a matter of fact, having to be out on the job in Africa in tropical rains necessitated special rainproof equipment, light and efficient, which rolls up into pocket-size packages. The weather's been too good here so far to need it, but I packed it today in case. As well as not liking to be a packhorse, I don't enjoy sleeping in wet clothes or shivering in a bivouac. You see, I don't do it the hardest way."

"Efficient, as always. Show me your route."

He pulled the map out of the pocket of his windcheater and traced the route for me, then stood up to go. I left my own lunch packet, windcheater and notebook where we had been sitting, and walked with him across the shaky wooden bridge, climbed up a long grassy slope and left him at the edge of the gully. He was taking what he said was a track across the middle of it, but all I could see were a few boulders, and then would climb up the rocky face on the far side, beyond which was another meadow, and thence a long trudge until the real climbing began. I watched him until he had climbed the rocky face opposite, which he did with seemingly little effort, but he was some distance away and I could not tell how difficult it really was. He turned and waved, then disappeared, and I went back to my base and my own programme, which was to stay there and have lunch and do some work, and go back to the car about tea-time unless I was too absorbed to bother about going back to the hotel for tea. As it happened, I was, and it was five o'clock when I finished writing and came back from my imaginary world to find that the sun had vanished, it was too late to get back for tea, and I was distinctly chilly.

I gathered my things together, and now having time in hand, I decided to warm myself up by exploring the gully, which might well figure in my plot. I could see some heavy clouds rolling up behind the mountains in the distance, but there seemed no imminent threat of rain, and I set about finding Gareth's track across the gully, which was invisible from the top. It was a scramble down, but once on the floor of the gully I could see the rocky track across, more like a small ledge in the smooth sweep down. I didn't much like the downward prospect, having a poor head for heights, but I kept my eyes on the rock face opposite and made my way to it. With a childish wish to see what was at the top of the cliff and trace Gareth's route to the peak, I tried to find his way up, but there seemed no visible way for me. The rock was fissured and I supposed a climber could find footholds easily enough in the cracks and on narrow ledges, but it was not easy enough for me to tackle, and moreover it was beginning to rain; big drops, like half crowns.

I zipped up my windcheater and skipped back across the gully as fast as I could. By the time I reached the rock face on the other side, it was coming down in sheets with a violence I had never known before. Reminding myself that cloudbursts seldom lasted long, I crouched under an overhanging rock and waited. It offered quite good protection, and I stayed there for some time, watching the rain sweep the gully. It obliterated the rock face opposite, and the scene was frightening in its fierce desolation. But this cloudburst showed no signs of exhausting itself, and in the end, chilled and damp, I decided I must get back to the stream and resign myself to a soaking. The climb up the rock on that side was fairly easy, and I thanked my lucky stars that I was wearing the canvas yachting shoes I had bought in Innsbruck which had rubber soles designed to grip wet decks, and which the saleswoman had assured me were excellent for rock climbing. At the top, I ran like a hare across the grassy slope down to the stream, the rain lashing my face, then pulled up with a shock of dismay. The stream was now a raging torrent and the wooden bridge had been swept away.

Too late, I realised my mistake in taking shelter under the rock for so long. I should have remembered the flimsy structure of the bridge. I stood there, taking stock, the rain still coming down in sheets and the stream, now a torrent, thundering along at my feet. Impossible to cross it. The force of the water would sweep me away like a twig. There was no possible way down along this side of the stream, for the drop became precipitous fifty yards along, and the upper reaches of the torrent showed no bridge and almost vertical climbing. I remembered when we had been studying the map that Gareth had said there was another way down on the far side of the gully to the next village along the road. It seemed the only solution to my predicament, but I didn't fancy crossing the gully again and the climb up the other side had looked too difficult for me. However, it was no time to quibble about difficulties. If I had to, I could doubtless climb that face Gareth had gone up so easily.

I glanced at my watch and was amazed to find it was nearly half past seven. I must have stayed under that rock longer than I'd realised. I hesitated no longer, and turned my face for the gully again. As always in the mountains, I had found, distances were deceptive, and now that I was tiring, the trudge up the grassy slope to the gully seemed much longer than before. The rain was not abating at all, but it was aimed at my back going this way and was not quite so blinding.

My heart sank when I at last reached the edge of the gully. Water was pouring down it carrying earth, stones and debris along with it. If I hesitated, this too would be impassable. I swarmed down the rocky face again, took my courage in my hands and half ran, half stumbled along the track, awash now but still offering some sort of foothold. But the prospect below me when I reached half-way was so frightening that I felt panic rise up in my throat and for one terrible moment I felt I must go down that swirling, dreadful water chute. I fought the panic and with a prayer in my heart waded and skipped and stumbled the rest of the way to the far cliff. There I leaned against a rock, trembling and weak, until I had regained control. If only, I thought, the noise would stop. The battering, tumultuous noise.

I could have been no wetter if I had just stepped out of a bath. The scarf I had tied round my head was sending rivulets of water down my back and my thin slacks clung to me like a second skin. I was half blinded by the rain and had given up trying to stem its cascades down my face. There came a time when you were so wet, it didn't matter. Like a half drowned cat, I prowled along the rock face trying to decide the easiest way up, but as water was cascading down it, masking what footholds and handholds there might be, I was forced to make a start at the first ledge I could see and hope it led to others. It was difficult to remember just where Gareth had gone, but I managed the first few yards without much difficulty. Then an overhang baulked me and I had to go round it, clinging with wet hands and straining toes to any crack or protuberance I could reach, thankful again for my non-slip rubbers which stood the test well. But about half-way up, I reached a large protruding slab over which the water fell as smooth as glass, and there seemed no way round. Nor any way back, for my last hoist up had sent the narrow rubble ledge from which I had pushed off crumbling away in the waterfall and only the fact that I had secured good handholds had saved me from falling. My toes were stuck in a narrow crack now as I searched despairingly for a way round this slab. Cautiously I edged along it and found a resting place about a foot square which joined the slab to the wall of the face again. It was solid rock and I rested on it thankfully for a few moments, my face pressed to the rock, gasping, aware that I was very tired.

When I had recovered a little, I examined the next pitch. It was as smooth and unbroken as a sheet of steel. Below me was air, for the face hollowed out there and it was a drop of about ten feet to the nearest rock below and that offered no foothold. I should merely bounce off down to the gully floor. If I edged back along the crack to the other side of the protruding slab, I was faced with a waterfall formed by a deep cleft. I was stuck.

I hardly knew how long I stayed there, numb and half stupefied. It suddenly seemed unreal. One read about other people being killed in accidents on holiday, but it could never be you. They were foolish people, taking unnecessary risks. But I had behaved like an idiot, too, not realising that rain of this intensity would be bound to turn a mountain stream into a torrent in no time at all. I had seen it happen in Scotland. And I had taken shelter for nearly an hour while it happened here and I was being cut off. Now I had about one square foot of wet rock to stand on until I grew too cold and too tired to hold myself on, or the water washed me off, for the whole rock face now resembled a waterfall. Nobody would see me here, and it was growing dark. And still the rain thundered down, deafening and blinding me.

I wondered where Gareth was. In the hut by now, I hoped. If the weather turns really sour, I shall turn back, he had said. Was there just a faint chance that he might be on the way down and see me? I took off my sodden headscarf which was serving no useful purpose and held it as well as I could against the protruding slab which had defeated me. It was white with a red pattern and might show up a little. Gareth, I thought. Gareth. And I closed my eyes and leaned my face against the rock, mingling tears with rain.

I don't know how long I stood there, eyes closed, cold and half drowned, despairing, thinking of Gareth and my father and Aunt Ella, and then, numbed, scarcely thinking at all, until a sharp sound jerked my eyes open and I saw a small rock bouncing away down the face a short distance to my right. I peered through the gloom, for the last light of that overcast evening was fast fading, and saw nothing. It was the rain washing down loosened rocks. Then above the sound of the rain, which seemed a little less fierce now, I heard a sharp chipping sound. An axe. Gareth appeared, roped, some way above me. He was not looking at me but studying the rock face left and right. Then he looked down and shouted:

"What a damned silly place to get stuck!"

Somehow, it was much more reassuring than any comforting words would have been.

"I know," I gasped, giddy with relief.

"You can't stay there like a praying mantis," he called. "I've got the rope secured and I'm going to drop the end to you. Tie it on just as I tell you."

The rope came snaking down and I tied it as he said, my cold wet fingers fumbling.

"Is there room on that ledge for me?" he said, peering down.

"No."

"Then check that knot. Did you tie it just as I said?"

"Yes. And it's secure."

"Right. Now listen. I'm going to lower you to the ledge immediately below you."

"There isn't one."

"Yes there is. That's a fairly deep hollow below you and the ledge at the foot is wide enough to hold a horse. I'll let the rope out slowly. Use your hands to steady yourself over the top. When you're down and secure, untie the rope, give me a good shout and stand well in. I'm coming to join you. Is that clear?"

"Yes," I said, looking at what looked a sheer drop beneath my feet down which the water was streaming.

"Right. Get moving."

Stiff and cold, I got down on my knees and gingerly lowered one leg over the drop.

"Take it easily," said Gareth. "You're quite safe. The rope's well belayed behind me and I could hold an elephant."

Reassured by this over-statement and the tautening rope, I lowered myself with my hands until I had to let go of the rock and hold the rope. After a few feet of being lowered like a bundle of washing, my feet found the ledge. In fact, the hollow beneath me was like a shallow cave and I went through a curtain of water to find myself in what was comparative shelter. I untied the rope, shouted up to Gareth and saw the rope disappear. A few minutes later, he came shinning down the doubled rope, coiling it up before coming through the curtain of water to join me.

"Well, Kate, how on earth did you land yourself in this fix?" he asked, putting a hand on my shoulder, the water streaming off his windcheater and waterproof trousers. He had on his head a kind of sou'wester which gave him a rakish look.

"I came across to explore the gully. I thought it would be useful for my plot. It started to rain and I took shelter for too long. When I got back to the stream it was a raging torrent and the bridge had gone. I came back to this side of the gully to try to get to the track down to the next village."

"But you said you were going back to the hotel for tea. It didn't start raining until this evening."

"I forgot the time, working. Thank heavens you saw me, Gareth! I don't think I could have stayed on much longer. I hadn't much hope. I thought you'd be spending the night in the mountain hut."

My voice was shaking and he put his arm round me as he said:

"I got there, but the weather looked so bad that it seemed more than doubtful that I could go for the peak tomorrow morning. I thought I'd just have time to get back before dark, and it was sheer luck that I saw your scarf. I was pretty certain I'd have to go down the other track. I thought the gully would be impassable, as well as the stream. I decided to take a look at it, though, and wondered what the white mark was on the rock. Thank goodness you had the sense to hang it out. I'd never have spotted you otherwise, and had no reason to think you weren't snugly back at the hotel."

"What are we going to do now? I'm no climber. I'll only make it dangerous for you."

"You haven't done so badly to get where you are. What have you got on your feet?"

He eyed the soles of my shoes and grunted, so that I didn't know whether he approved or not.

"Should I stay here while you go for help?" I asked, shivering.

"Good grief, no! It's only a scramble up to the top, with the help of the rope and the axe. But we must get moving while there's still a glimmer of light. We'll rope up. All you have to do is follow me, keep your eye on the holds I use, and move when I say so. If you slip, I can hold you. I shan't let you move until I'm secured. Nothing to worry about. Move lightly and get balanced. Think of it more like dancing movements than desperate clutches."

He tied me on the rope, and I steeled myself to leave the meagre shelter and face the wet, slippery rocks again. Gareth took a diagonal line, finding cracks and handholds, twice using the axe driven into a crack which was too narrow for fingers to grasp, and at one precarious hold using it similarly to belay the rope behind him. He moved lightly, rhythmically, but by no stretch of the imagination could I liken this to dancing and I crept up clinging desperately with fingers and toes, telling myself that if I fell, Gareth might well fall, too, despite his assurances, for the streaming water made all holds treacherous, even for nailed boots. Having Gareth there with me, however, made an enormous difference to my confidence, and we got to within about nine feet of the top without the rope having once tightened uncomfortably between us. Gareth stopped on a ledge there. I was a few feet below.

"The next step's too big for you, Kate. I'll go to the top, belay the rope and haul you up this bit. All right?"

I nodded, and using his axe for a hold he swung off to the right and disappeared over the top. It was now almost dark and he was only a black shape above me as he called down.

"Use your feet to keep yourself balanced away from the face and hang on to the rope with your hands. No hurry."

He hauled me steadily up the last pitch until I lay floundering on the top like a landed fish.

"Well done," he said, and helped me to my feet.

In the last glimmer of light I could make out a sloping pasture and vague black heights through the curtain of rain.

"It's too dark to take you down tonight, Kate. There's one steep rocky pitch on the way. I wouldn't fancy it myself in the dark, and I certainly can't risk it with you. We'll have to shack up for the night."

"Where?" I asked, thinking that the moon could not have offered a less inviting prospect.

"I passed a hut on my way down. Not a mountain refuge. Some sort of herdsman's shelter. Rough, but dry. It's our only choice, I'm afraid."

"Is it far?"

"Across this pasture, where it becomes bare rock. No climbing. About half an hour's slog. All right?"

I nodded, put my head down and plodded after him like a tired old horse, forcing one leg in front of the other, my calf muscles protesting all the way, the relentless rain driving against us now and making me wonder whether it would ever stop. Gareth, glistening in the darkness like a seal in front of me, turned once or twice to make sure I was still there, but set a steady unrelenting pace.

When I stumbled after him into the hut, I was too spent to do anything but sink to the floor, thankful at last to be out of the tumult and misery of the rainstorm.

Gareth's torch flickered round and fastened on a lantern. From the recesses of his clothing he found a lighter.

"We're in luck; this candle's almost new."

The lantern filled the hut with a comforting if dim light. While Gareth removed his windcheater and waterproofs and piled them in a corner, I looked round, still unable to move. The hut would just about have been large enough to house Gareth's car, with a bench along one side, a small roughly made trestle table, and a pile of straw in one corner. But it must have been well built, for it was quite dry except for a small patch of wet where the rain had driven in under the four-pane window in the side opposite me.

"Welcome to this luxurious apartment," said Gareth with a little smile as he held out his hands to pull me to my feet. I left a pool of water behind me and it still dripped from my windcheater.

Gareth had come through the weather remarkably well, justifying the claims of his tropical waterproofs. His ski pants and sweater were dry; only his boots were sodden and the front of his hair hung damply on his forehead. I was wet through to the skin. If I had been a climber, experience would have taught me something about equipment. As it was, my thin windcheater, silk scarf, drip-dry slacks and cotton shirt were about as effective as tissue paper against such violent weather.

"You'll have to get out of those clothes," said Gareth. "You can have my spare sweater and socks."

He unstrapped his knapsack and drew out an oilskin roll which contained a thick green sweater and a pair of grey woollen socks.

"I reckon they'll just about cover you," he said, with a grin.

"While you change, I'll see what food I can rustle up. Have you got anything in that bag?"

I had slung my shoulder bag round my shoulder under my windcheater, and I was a little relieved to be able to produce something that had withstood the rain, for its zipped-up exterior was of a washable plastic material, and my precious notebook, odds and ends, and the remnants of my lunch were all dry.

"Four biscuits and one and a half sausage rolls. I didn't care for the sausage, so I only ate a half."

"You'll like it when you're hungry. I've got two apples, a bar of chocolate and a couple of cheese rolls, so we shan't starve. And this," he added triumphantly, bringing out a Thermos flask.

"Not coffee?" I said hopefully.

"The very same. Only about half full, though, so we can't exactly indulge. And give yourself a rub down with this," he said, handing me a rough but clean piece of terry towelling.

"You think of everything," I said, beginning to feel better.

"I went prepared to sleep out for a night. You look like a poor pinched little orphan of the storm. Get changed. I'll spare you any embarrassment by concentrating on the victuals."

I stripped hastily down to my briefs, rubbed myself down and pulled on Gareth's sweater. It reached to the middle of my thighs, and the soft Shetland wool was as comforting as a glowing fire on a January day. The sleeves were far too long and I rolled them back. The woollen socks reached nearly to my knees. I began to stop shivering, and towelled my hair vigorously.

Gareth had spread out the food and was now removing his boots.

"I've kept two biscuits and the apples for the morning," he said, "and we'd better keep back half of the coffee. That's quite a natty outfit," he added, surveying me with a quizzical expression. "I've seen shorter mini-skirts."

"It's cosy. Bless you. Nothing like being drenched to lower one's morale. I begin to feel hungry."

I had propped my mirror on the window ledge and was trying to restore some order to my hair. Gareth was wiping his hands on the damp towel. When I looked reasonably civilised again, I picked up my shirt and slacks and wrung them out from the doorway, then draped them over one end of the bench. I shook out Gareth's waterproof trousers and windcheater and did the same with them.

We decided to save until the end the small cup of coffee each which was all we had to spare, and started on the sausage roll and a half. Gareth was right. The sausage tasted good now. We followed up with the chocolate, then the cheese rolls. The coffee was sheer bliss. In the lantern light, that bare hut seemed like paradise after the experiences of the past few hours. I was so happy and thankful that I could only beam at Gareth as I sipped that delectable coffee. The rain drumming on the roof only added to my sense of comfort. Do your worst, I thought.

And then tiredness took over and I could hardly keep my eyes open.

"That candle won't last indefinitely," said Gareth, opening the lantern and inspecting it. "We shall want it in the morning. Best get some sleep now."

Dopily, I collected the wrappings of our food while Gareth inspected the straw in the corner and shook it up.

"It's reasonably clean and I've known worse mattresses," he said, patting it. "If we're not to get too cold for comfort, we'll need each other's warmth. Settle yourself in while I close down for the night."

In my state of tiredness, even hard floor-boards would have been welcome, and the straw was surprisingly comfortable. I turned on my side, and Gareth put the ground sheet over me and blew the candle out. He lay down beside me, curving himself round my back, saying:

"One back will have to be cold. It had better be mine."

I snuggled against him, at peace with the world.

"Good-night, Gareth. Thank you for ... everything," I murmured for I was too drowsy to pick my words.

I didn't hear his reply, for I went out like the candle.

16

A Time to Talk

WHEN I AWOKE, wondering where on earth I was, I found myself alone.

"Gareth," I said.

A dim shape in the doorway turned and I saw the glowing end of a cigarette. I was aware of the silence. The rain had stopped.

"Hullo. You seem to have slept well," he observed as he threw the end of the cigarette away, closed the door and lit the lantern.

I peered at my watch through bleary eyes. It was half past two.

"Another hour to sunrise, when we can start back," he said. "I suggest we have breakfast in bed, since it's warmer there and this bench is singularly hard. How do you feel?"

"Fine. Did I say fine?" I added as I sat up and moved my stiff legs, which were hostile to movement, to say the least.

"The first day's the worst."

"I'd like a wash before breakfast. Where's that towel?"

"Here. And no shortage of water. There's a pool in a rock outside that's big enough to bath in. Take my torch."

I wriggled into my still damp shoes, every movement painful. Outside, the air was cold and sweet, and in the night sky a few stars were glimmering between the clouds. The rain-water was soft and refreshing, and I felt wide awake when I returned to find that Gareth had piled some of the straw against the wall to form a soft back, and was measuring out the coffee.

We sat on our improvised couch and had our ration of coffee with a biscuit and an apple apiece. It all tasted surprisingly good.

"We've got about an hour to wait, then?" I said, munching my apple.

"M'm. We'll get moving as soon as it's light, before the search parties set out. They won't be bothered about me because they'll assume I spent the night at the hut, but they'll be worried about you."

"While we're waiting," I said carefully, "do you think we might have that talk?"

There was an odd little pause, then he said quietly:

"Well, we shan't have any interruptions. And it's long overdue."

"When I wrote that letter, Gareth," I said jerkily, "I couldn't give you a chance to reply because you would have talked me round. You always did. And I knew I had to do what I did. Every word I wrote in that letter was true, wrung out of my mind even though it mangled my heart."

"How much were you influenced by Janet's talk?"

"Not much. Oh, I know I flew off the handle about the girl, and you said beastly things about my being jealous and petty-minded, but we'd both lost our tempers, and underneath, it was about far more than your having dinner with a girl. I told you that in the letter, which was not written in anger. Janet perhaps provided the match for the bonfire, but I had a whole box of matches waiting."

"You should have given me the chance to explain about the girl, anyway. I was too angry that night."

"It wasn't important. I knew you weren't the philandering type. It just seemed the last straw in the load that made it impossible for me to go on yoked to it. What was the explanation, anyway?"

"She was my secretary. She'd forfeited her Easter week-end to come with me to the conference on the motorway crisis. I needed her to make the report. We got back on the Monday evening. The least I could do was give the girl a good dinner before she went home."

"Of course. But it wasn't really about that. If you read the letter, you must have realised that."

"If I read the letter!" said Gareth bitterly. "It's worn out with reading. I admit I was a good deal to blame, but you weren't blameless either. You were always so anxious to do what I wanted, to be loving and agree with anything I planned, that I naturally began to take you for granted."

"But when I tried to stand on my own feet, you always got round me. You always had that weapon of physical attraction and you used it."

"Who wouldn't? But I didn't know you as well as I thought I did, Kate. I saw you as a delightful, loving girl who needed a strong arm to protect her. You lacked confidence in yourself, you weren't tough in any sense, and I saw myself as your protector. I was going to look after you, always. I was wrong in stopping you from taking that job. I wanted you to be available whenever I was free. That was selfish. I admit it. But I also thought you'd find the London world of journalism a tough one. Too tough for you. I didn't realise that underneath the gentle exterior was a different Kate Danville struggling to get out."

"One that wouldn't suit your book nearly as well?"

He shifted restlessly while he thought about this one.

"I agree that I was as vain and possessive and selfish as many young men might be in love with a girl so yielding and so very much in love. But we grow up."

"You were twenty-six. I was only twenty."

"That only made me think I should take charge of you. Your letter and your determination not to see me again brought me up with a shock, I can tell you. When I'd got over being angry, I set about digging out the truth, examining how it had happened, because I knew we loved each other, I knew we belonged, and I couldn't believe it was ended. And I had a chat with Aunt Ella which threw a little light on your, to me, astonishing behaviour."

"Aunt Ella? When?"

"Oh, about two months after your flight, when I tried for the last time to get your address out of her. She wouldn't give it to me because she'd promised you, but she told me about your childhood. How your mother had robbed you of all confidence by her continual denigration. True?"

"Yes. My parents' marriage wasn't a happy one. When you're a child you don't understand these things. You take it all for granted. It's only of late years, looking back, that I've realised just how much of a failure it was. My mother took refuge in being an invalid. A psychosomatic invalid, the doctor said. My father took refuge in an ironical detachment. I think my mother was jealous of his affection for me. Anyway, that's how it was. I was seventeen when Mother was killed in a road accident. And Aunt Ella came to keep house for us. By then I possessed the biggest inferiority complex going, until you came along and actually preferred me to any other girl, and I was bowled over. And what little individuality I possessed was swamped by a much stronger one; yours. When I ran away, I was running for my life, for the chance of finding myself."

"That's what Aunt Ella said. She thought I'd be wise to give you time to do it, if I could school myself to such patience. When I pointed out that time would put a gulf between us, would inevitably take us apart, she said I'd have to take that risk. All this came out in her usual random way, sandwiched in between chat about the garden and your parents and a tame robin."

"I can imagine," I said, smiling. "I'm often amazed at the shrewd little observations which dart in and out of the babbling stream of Aunt Ella's words like minnows. She's the most deceptive person I know. I've learned not to underrate her. You were always her blue-eyed boy, of course. Just how did you know I was going to be here? It wasn't accident, of course."

"No. I had a pact with Aunt Ella. I promised not to ferret you out if she'd promise to let me know if and when you showed signs of marrying anyone else. She kept her promise. I'd just got back from Africa when she wrote a delightfully chatty letter to me at the office with the news that you were coming here for a month, during which you were going to come to a decision about marrying John Castleford, who was accompanying you for the first week. She rather thought his chances were good. A worthy man, she said."

"So that was it! Shortly before I came away she produced an old snapshot of you. She'd found it in a book, she said, ever so casually. Did I want it? Subtle. That's Aunt Ella."

"And did you want it?"

"I tore it up and buried the pieces under the hawthorn tree, reminding myself that freedom was splendid and that those emotion-ridden days had reduced me to a pathetic object, as Janet reminded me on Sunday."

"I see," said Gareth grimly.

"What did you expect when you came here, Gareth? That I would fly to your arms again with an expression of joy?"

"I shouldn't have learned anything if I'd thought that, should I? No. I wanted to find out whether I was mistaken in thinking that what was between us was indestructible. It was fortuitous that I'd just been ordered a month's sick leave. I thought, directly I see Kate, I shall know. Four years is a long time. I might find a stranger. But I knew, immediately I saw you sitting under the tree eating that apple on the way here, that I felt the same. And I knew from the expression on your face when you first caught sight of me in the courtyard that morning that I hadn't become a stranger to you, either. Whatever else it was that looked out of your face, it wasn't boredom or indifference, though you tried hard to make out that it was. That first moment was too revealing, Kate. I had the advantage of you. I saw you unprepared."

"Yes. I didn't recognise you as you scorched by on that first morning, shattering my peace with your horn. I might have guessed!"

"You were badly parked and the offside door was ajar. I thought somebody might emerge if I didn't give a warning. Then I saw you calmly sitting under the tree."

"I'd have thought you were going too fast to recognise anybody."

"Not recognise that chestnut hair and the way you hold your head? I'd know it anywhere. And I wasn't altogether unprepared. I knew from Aunt Ella that you drove a Morris. *Would* you have said yes to Castleford, Kate?"

"I'd almost decided to when I came away. But here, everything seemed different. He's a good friend, but I found out that it was on such a superficial level that marriage was out of the question. I'm sure he realised that, too, before the week was out. It is, I suppose, a business friendship. I'd been living at that nice shallow level for the past two years, anyway. You jerked me into deep water as soon as you appeared, although I struggled."

"And how! But why did you behave in that idiotic fashion, as though we were strangers, when that first encounter spelt out so plainly that we weren't? You couldn't imagine I'd settle for that."

"I was afraid, again, of being put back where I was when we split up. The same attraction was there. The same force. I felt ... threatened. It was cowardly. I see that now."

"It was foolish to think I'd try to force you into anything, Kate. What happiness would there be for either of us in that? But surely, as two adults, we can talk over what went wrong and see if we can do better, because I can't bear to lose you without making that effort. I almost gave up when you accused me of wanting to get my own back. I thought then that I'd been mistaken, that there *was* a gulf between us, after all, if you could think I was that kind of a person. But you took that back, and since then I've fancied you've changed your attitude. Have you?"

"I did what you said you did; tried to be quite detached and dig out the truth, because I'd been in a state of panicky confusion ever since you arrived on the scene. In an odd way, though, this holiday's taught me things I didn't know about myself and about you. The people I've met here. It's hard to explain."

"Try. I want to understand, Kate."

"Well, the business with Max Corinth in my room did more to open my eyes about John Castleford than anything. No need to go into that. But that nasty incident with Mrs Chagford's bag brought you to my rescue, and made me realise that I wasn't so clever, and I was glad of your support. Then Ann reminded me of myself when young and I saw how inevitable it was that you should master me, order my life when I was so patently inadequate and vulnerable. And I thought how good you were with

Roger, and with Miss Courtland. It seemed to me that you'd changed since those early days. And I've talked a bit with Monsieur Corbeil, and he's helped me to sort myself out. Janet contributed, too, because although she gave me some nasty knocks, her reminders of those final stages of our engagement weren't so ravaging as they would have been even two years ago, so that I realised, perhaps for the first time, that I wasn't that vulnerable, uncertain child any more. I'd found myself, and the clock couldn't be put back. I didn't think about all this at the time, but on Sunday something happened that brought me to the moment of truth."

"I knew something was different on Sunday night. What happened, then? Janet again?"

"No, nothing like that. She left in the morning. It was that car accident. I was on the hill above and I saw the aftermath and the stretcher. I thought it was you. The car was the same as yours. I couldn't read the number plate on it. Everybody had gone by the time I got to it, and I didn't know it wasn't your car until I got back to the hotel car park and saw it there. I think that was the worst half hour I've ever lived through. That was what pulled me up with something more than a jerk."

"Poor Kate. You can't be happy with the devil alive, and you can't bear him dead. What's to be done?" asked Gareth as he drew me to him.

"Well," I said unsteadily, "I think I'm confident enough now to hold my own with him in partnership, if he still wants me."

"That qualification is unnecessary, as you well know. I love you, Kate. I always did. But now more than ever, when I know you better and know myself better. I think we can strike a balance now and make a good thing of marriage."

"Yes. There's no peace for either of us, it seems, otherwise."

He took my face between his hands and searched it intently.

"Say it, Kate," he said quietly.

"I love you, Gareth. I was in love with you before. Now I love you so deeply that I wanted to die when I thought you were dead. I'm sorry it's taken me so long to discover that, but I think the years between were necessary."

"Yes. So do I. Though I don't intend to give you any more time to think about it. Special licence directly we get back?"

"So urgent?"

"So urgent."

"Agreed," I said, and he took me in his arms then and it was some time before we had any breath for words.

A thin light was showing through the window when he finally released me and came back to practicalities, saying cheerfully:

"There never was anything wrong with the chemistry, anyway."

"Too true. You must have felt confident, to make that bargain with me and not use such a strong weapon. Except, of course, that it was there all the time."

He laughed as he pulled me to my feet and removed some straw from my hair.

"That was my low cunning. My yielding, gentle love had turned into a formidable adversary calling for all the wily tactics I could think up."

"You're still going to need them. The gentle dove has gone."

"You're telling me! It won't be dull, anyway. I rather like a good scrap, and think how nice the reconciliations will be."

I rubbed his black hair, feeling as happy and confident as a lark, and kissed him again.

"I hate having to break this up, but we'd better get moving," he said, after another interval. "That's a seductive outfit, but hardly good climbing kit. Do you think those slacks of yours are dry?"

I hobbled over to the bench and felt them. They were still damp.

"They'll be all right if I pull them over these long socks and tuck the sweater in."

"You don't look capable of climbing off a soap box at the moment," said Gareth. "Here, put your foot up on the bench."

He pulled down each sock in turn and rubbed my calf muscles, which felt like wood.

"They'll feel better when you get warm," he said, and blew out the lantern. "Better leave some Austrian schillings to pay for another candle. There's only half an inch of this one left."

"Do you think it's used much? This hut?"

"In bad weather, maybe. The herdsmen live pretty rough on these high pastures during the summer. In winter, it's probably handy as a skiers' refuge."

"Well, we've reason to be grateful for it. I'll pen a note of thanks in my best German, which isn't very good."

We collected our belongings, and left the hut as we had found it with the exception of some schillings by the lantern and a sheet of my notebook on which I had printed *Danksagung für Schutz*, and signed it *Zwei Brittischen Besucher* in deference to the half of Gareth that was Welsh.

It was cold and grey as we started down across the pasture, but by the time we had reached the rocky pitch Gareth had mentioned, the sun was breaking through. We roped up and I found it difficult, with stiff limbs and chilled fingers. Gareth was firm, paying no attention when I niggled at a long stride, and making my hair stand on end when he drove his axe into a cleft and stood on the handle while he guided and then held my foot into a niche above him which I declared was invisible. When we were down, he grinned and said:

"Not bad, in the circumstances. We'll make a climber of you yet."

"Never," I declared. "I shall stay in the meadows and pick flowers."

As we proceeded on our way down, the desolation left by the previous night's storm became more apparent, with uprooted trees and scoured water-courses down which earth and rubble had shifted. Gareth surveyed the scene with foreboding.

"It's worse than I expected. I'm wondering what's happened to your car, Kate. Right at the bottom of that gully."

"I'd forgotten that."

"The rain seems to have shifted tons of earth. An avalanche of earth instead of snow. Hope none of the villages below were in the path of it."

The track through the last stretch of pine wood was slithery and treacherous, and I barked my hand catching at a tree-trunk round the last hair-pin bend. We could hear men's voices and the sound of shovels. When we came out on to the road, we found it blocked a few yards away by a mountain of earth and rubble, and men at work clearing it. Gareth, whose German was better than mine, had a few words with them.

"The road's blocked in two places," he said when he rejoined me. "Thousands of tons of soil came down, apparently. Only one village suffered, and there it was fortunately only parked cars that were the casualties. Communications and power supplies are all up the pole, though."

"Our hopes of thumbing a lift along the road to my car are pretty dim, then. Even supposing the car's still there."

"I'm afraid it was right in the path of another fall, because the stuff came down that gully like a cataract, so one of the men said. They're due there after they've dealt with this little lot."

"Do you think the hotel will be all right?"

"Yes. Protected by the woods behind. The stream probably flooded, but even so, I doubt whether it would have affected the hotel. The slope of the land would see to that."

We trudged along the road until we reached the gully where I had left my car. All that could be seen was a great pile of earth and rocky rubble completely blocking the road and spilling off over the low stone wall into the ravine below. Gareth whistled.

"This looks bad, Kate. Wait here. I'll scout around."

He clambered round the perimeter of the pile of earth and mud to the stone wall and peered over. If my car wasn't under the pile of earth on the gully side, it would have been pushed over the road with the force of the rocks and earth and down into the ravine. And indeed this was what had happened.

"It's down there," said Gareth, scrambling back. "A write-off, I'm afraid, Kate. You were insured?"

"Yes."

"Come round here. You can just see it."

He helped me over a pile of rubble to the wall and I leaned over. The car was upside down, smashed up against a rock, a complete wreck.

"Well, that's that. Still, if empty cars are the only casualties, there's not much to grieve over," I said.

"True. Someone's been down to make sure that it was empty, by the look of those tracks down there, but we'll notify the authorities as soon as we can, anyway."

We had to make a weary detour to cross the ravine, and it was nearly half past seven when we walked up the hotel track. We had been nearly four hours getting back.

"Oh, for a hot bath and an English breakfast of bacon and eggs!" I said.

"Oh for a shave! I feel like a hedgehog."

"Well, you don't look like one. Slightly brigandish, that's all. The hotel seems to have kept out of trouble."

Franz came hurrying out as we approached.

"*Gott sei dank!* The maid who takes the early tea has just reported that your bed was not slept in, Miss Danville. We had not noticed your absence last night, when the lights went out and there was a call for help from the village, because the river was flooding, and all was confusion. What a night! You are all right?"

"Quite all right, thank you, Franz. We sheltered in a hut. Just tired and dirty and hungry. What about the village?"

"Not much damage. We were able to reinforce the danger spot on the river bank in time. And now we must get you a good breakfast," he said, beaming with relief.

As we went upstairs, Gareth said:

"If we're nippy, we may beat the lazybones to the bathrooms."

We were, and we did. We met at breakfast, civilised again, and I shared Gareth's table.

"If you think I'm going to have any more meals looking at your back, you're mistaken," he said, holding the chair for me.

"Darling," I said, "if you're going to drive me home on Thursday, promise me you won't scorch."

"I never scorch, unless it's safe. But I'll promise to go no faster than thirty if my lady commands."

"That would be the day! I'll settle for a maximum of sixty, when safe."

"We'll allow plenty of time, then," said Gareth, smiling wickedly.

"I shall telephone my father and Aunt Ella tonight. Won't they be surprised? They're expecting me to come home engaged, but to a certain John Castleford."

"Never can tell with these fickle types. A worthy man, too, as Aunt Ella said. Trust her to hit on the right adjective."

"John would make a splendid husband. So reliable. And he would *never* make me climb down precipices."

"A little dull, though, don't you think?"

"Well... No star-shine, anyway."

"Can't have it all ways. That looks good, Lise."

In view of our night out, our breakfast had been considerably fortified, and as well as the customary coffee, rolls, marmalade and butter, there were some Frankfurters with grated horse-radish, and some slices of ham and cheese.

"Will that be enough?" asked the fair-haired little waitress hesitantly.

"Just right, I'd say," said Gareth.

And never had breakfast tasted so good. And never had two people been so happy, I thought as I poured out Gareth's third cup of coffee and we continued to babble light-hearted nonsense as though we had imbibed nothing but champagne. Perhaps it was reaction from the previous night's drama, perhaps relief at having found our way back to each other, perhaps the sheer magic of loving and being loved again, but we were neither of us quite sober at that breakfast table and could have made sense to nobody but each other.

17

Falcon Recaptured

RESTED, AND WITH the formalities of the accident to my car attended to, we spent the afternoon quietly in a meadow on the lower slopes of the hill behind the hotel. It was a fine, warm afternoon, and it was hard to believe that the storm of the previous night was not a figment of our imaginations, for apart from the over-full stream and the softness of the ground, this meadow, protected by the contours of the land behind, looked shining and green and peaceful, and saxifrages were blooming unharmed in nooks among the rocks. We had spread the groundsheet on the grass at the foot of a conveniently shaped boulder, and had managed to bring ourselves back to a state sober enough to discuss practical matters.

"This special licence," I said. "Where do we live?"

"Temporarily, your flat or mine. I've got mine on a quarterly basis. It's fairly capacious, in a quiet part of Kensington. What's yours like?"

"Too small for two. It had better be yours."

"Eventually, I thought, we might like a house in the country. Near enough to London to commute. About two years ago I bought a plot of land in Surrey. Haven't done anything with it yet. Nice position, on the North Downs looking across the weald."

"What made you buy it? Your work keeps you on the move so much."

"I always fancied a base in the country. Anyway, a friend of our senior partner was selling off part of his estate separately. He was a business tycoon, about to retire and move to the Channel Islands. The mansion was bought by a film star, but this four-acre site, with planning permission for a private residence, was sold separately and I thought it was too good an opportunity to let slip. Even if I didn't want it myself, its value would increase. So I bought it. A good place for writing."

"Sounds wonderful." I looked at him thoughtfully. Just how confident had he been?

"I know a good architect. We could probably get a house built within the year. That is, if the site appeals to you. We'll go and have a look at it as soon as we get back. Will you feel like keeping on with the Danville Typing Service if it involves so much travelling, though?"

"I'd planned to withdraw gradually as soon as I could, to concentrate on writing. I shall keep an eye on it for a year or two, though. Perhaps go up once a month, until Joyce—she's my assistant—is happy to take over on her own."

"I suppose I shall be known as the husband of the famous author," said Gareth, his eyes teasing me.

"I doubt it."

"How's the new book coming on?"

"It's suffered from too many distractions."

"Too bad. Well, wait until you're settled in a quiet retreat in Surrey with a loving husband, and you'll be able to concentrate like mad. We might be able to get Willie to come and give you a hand with the housekeeping so that you've more time for your own work. She's retired to a cottage near there."

"You mean Mrs Wilton, who used to keep house for you and your father?"

"The very same. After the old man died and I sold the house, we kept in touch."

"I was sorry when I heard about your father. That was a few months after I left home. Did you move to London after that? I never asked at home and they never mentioned your name. I asked them not to. You see, I had to try to forget, and it was so hard."

"You're forgiven. Yes, I wanted to get away from Bray Hill. It was full of painful memories for me, too. And work was pressing. It seemed sensible to live nearer the office. Work was a good anodyne."

"That's what I found. And I came to enjoy it, too. When you sent me that telegram about my book, you didn't try to get in touch with me again."

"I was too deeply involved in the African job. It was only a flying visit back to the office to report. I had no time, and my partner in crime told me that you were all set on being a career woman and that there was no immediate risk of your being carried off by another man. She thought the time was still not ripe."

I turned to him then and said slowly:

"Did you *never* accept that we had parted for good, then?"

"That's the sixty-four dollar question," said Gareth, plucking a piece of grass and studying it intently. "One bit of me never accepted it, although heaven knows you made it seem final enough. But in my heart, I felt we belonged. And I'm a persistent devil. I don't like being beaten."

"You're telling me! I'm glad, though," I said, kissing him. "I don't know why some girl hasn't snapped you up in the meantime."

"Nobody appealed like you. Funny, isn't it? You're nice to look at, but I've known more beautiful females. You once had a beautiful docile nature, too, and now you're tough and independent. And yet even now I only have to see you come into a room, to watch the way you walk, the tilt of your head, to feel my bones melt and my heart go all mushy."

"Is that how it takes you? With me, it's more like an electric shock. That dark, handsome, menacing face, I think; I must fly before I'm enslaved. And all the time I'm edging up to you, all of a tingle."

He laughed and drew me down in the circle of his arm, saying:

"It's no good. There's something in this mountain air that makes it impossible to plan soberly."

"It could be love."

"So it could. Anyway, we'll settle all the details when we get home. The only thing that is fixed is that within a week of our arrival, you will be Mrs Ferrion."

"So precipitate," I said, shaking my head.

Then our mood changed and we stopped fooling as he pulled me to him roughly, saying in a smothered voice:

"I want you, Kate, and I've waited a long time."

"I'll make up for that, my love," I said. "I promise."

And as his hands and lips went roving, it was sweet to surrender to that sphere of his domination that had always been absolute and which I had never challenged nor wished to challenge.

When I telephoned home that evening, Aunt Ella did not seem unduly surprised at my news, though clearly delighted.

"How very nice, dear. I always did like that young man. So *different*. And however much you may like being free, a companion through life is a great help ... someone to drive the car ... yes, I know you like driving yourself, but I'm sure you'll manage splendidly ... so effective, Gareth ... I hope Mr Castleford wasn't too disappointed ... Not the sort to fret, I'm sure ... Gareth is bringing you home? ... He must stay the rest of the week-end ... I'll fetch your father."

My father's voice seemed even more calm and deliberate than usual after Aunt Ella's breathless babble.

"Bless you, dear Kate. I hope you'll both be very happy. You know my views on matrimony, but if you must enter those stormy waters, I quite frankly prefer Gareth as a son-in-law to that other chap ... Not altogether surprised since from your aunt's stream-of-consciousness talk lately I seem to have heard Gareth's name once or twice connected with the hotel you're staying at ... Too clever by half, I agree ... It will be good to see you both ... Is Gareth there?"

I handed the telephone to Gareth, who participated in one of those irritatingly cryptic conversations which reveal absolutely nothing to the listener. He was laughing when he rang off, but said the Greek quotation was not fit for my ears, and when pressed merely added that my father seemed resigned to losing me and reasonably pleased with my choice.

And then it was our last day in Mölden, culminating in a little dinner party in the evening at a restaurant in Innsbruck arranged by Monsieur Corbeil to celebrate our engagement.

"And so the falconer has his falcon captive again on his wrist," he said to me with a little smile as we waited for Gareth to bring the car round.

"I'm afraid so."

"And you wear the bloom of love, which is very nice even for an old cynic like me to see."

The restaurant was a gourmet's delight, and Monsieur Corbeil toasted us in a vintage white wine which even my inexperienced palate could appreciate as something special. Afterwards, he said, with a gleam in his eyes:

"She has suffered much in her struggles to escape, your Kate. And I thought, how awful, those times when we are in love. I am glad not to be young again. And now I see her face, and yours, Gareth, and I am not so glad. It is a madness; but how delightful! And she had to think you dead, the little falcon, before she realised her destiny."

"And what good would her wreaths have been to me?" said Gareth.

"Exactly. What did he say? Your English poet.

'The grave's a fine and private place,
But none I think do there embrace.'

She realised that, I think, your Kate, when she ran past me like a terrified ghost. There was I, walking peacefully up the track to the hotel, when this wraith went by at the speed of light. I followed as best I could, to find her weeping over your car in a state of collapse."

This story had lost nothing in the telling, for Monsieur Corbeil was something of an actor, and I said crisply:

"Well, anybody would have been the same, thinking a friend had suffered that fate."

"You see," said Gareth, smiling at me, "even now she's afraid to give me an inch."

"She has given you much more than an inch, my friend, or

you would not look as you do. I have seen you looking like a smouldering volcano. Now it is all calm satisfaction. It is well. I like to see happy faces round me. There are not so many these days."

"You enjoy being an observer," said Gareth.

"It is a rôle forced on me. But I enjoy it, yes. The guests in the hotel I have found most interesting. And you two, the most interesting of all. Your friend who came for the first week, Kate. Now I found him a typical cold-blooded, reserved Englishman. They are like that, I thought. Then came this one." He nodded at Gareth. "Do the English come like this, too? I said to myself. Passionate, dangerous, determined."

It was my turn to smile at Gareth.

"It's the Welsh half of him," I explained.

"Ah, the Celtic strain. That accounts for it, chérie. You will have a job handling it, perhaps. But much happiness, I am sure."

I thought it time to divert Monsieur Corbeil to other members of our hotel party, and asked him what he had thought of Max Corinth. During the rest of the evening, he amused us by the shrewdness of his judgments on the others. Never unkind, but never cosy, either, he dissected with a skilled knife. He was a brave man, I thought, and a rare one, to be able to spend the last months of his life in such a calm, detached frame of mind, interested still in his fellow humans, unembittered, unafraid, his sense of humour still intact. And I was sad, too, and embraced him warmly when we said good-night in the courtyard of the hotel. He must have sensed how I was feeling, for he patted my shoulder and said:

"It comes to all of us, Kate. I am lucky in the way it is coming to me, without much pain. I shall carry your happy face with me on the rest of my travels. Au revoir."

When Monsieur Corbeil left us, Gareth said:

"What about driving up the pass and saying our good-bye to the mountains there? I never showed you that view, since you were base enough to drive off in my car when my back was turned."

He handled the car beautifully up the pass, and I was just thinking how much better he was at it than I, when he said:

"You still give me an old-fashioned look occasionally, as though doubting my reformed character, so may I be allowed to reassure you by replacing that symbol of independence, your car? A suitable gift from groom to bride in the circumstances, don't you think?"

"Very suitable, and most generous. Thank you, darling. Can I choose it?"

"Well, I hope you'll allow me to advise you."

I gurgled delightedly and he pulled my ear as I said:

"I had a feeling you thought you could do better."

"Well, cars have moved on since the year yours was made, you know."

"Pay no heed. You shall choose. I know nothing about them, anyway, and am only concerned to have something that will move me from place to place and not break down."

Gareth shook his head at this regrettable attitude and brought the Mercedes to a gentle halt in the parking place. We got out and walked up the road to the bend, our footsteps ringing out in the quiet night. We had come a long way, I thought, since that last excursion here.

"What a fantastic holiday this has been!" I said. "I still wonder if I've dreamed it all."

"You seem real enough to me," said Gareth, his arm round my waist.

"I suppose I'll collect myself when I get back, but I still feel in a beautiful trance."

"I think I'll take you back to that hawthorn tree and make you dig up the pieces of that snapshot and paste them together again. But on second thoughts, perhaps not. That failure is best buried. We'll concentrate on the future."

"It looks good to me," I said, as we stood gazing over the foothills and valleys to the high mountains beyond, their snow-covered peaks silvered by the moon.

"We were about a third of the way up that one with the crinkly ridge two nights ago."

We fell silent, the majesty of the scene making any words seem inadequate. A feeling of perfect peace enveloped me then. Perhaps I had supped too full of emotions during these holiday weeks, and now rested in a state of tranquillity. Perhaps Gareth felt the same, for we stayed there for some time, his arm round my shoulders, in silence. A state of grace. Now I knew what those words meant.

18

Postscript

PERHAPS IT WAS Ann who said the last word about it when she came to spend the day with us soon after we had moved into our house in Surrey. As we might have expected, delays in planning and building upset all our calculations and we did not move in until the autumn of the following year, so that it was a calm, sunny day in late October when Ann paid her first visit there.

We were pleased with the house. The architect had found some mellow red bricks for it and had designed it in a style which suited its rural surroundings. There were some fine old oak and ash trees on one boundary of what would be our garden, but which was now a large field sloping away from the house, and a hedgerow ran round the rest of the boundary which was low enough not to impede the view across the weald to the South Downs.

Ann thought it beautiful and expressed her approval in her usual honest, ingenuous fashion. It was one of her endearing qualities, this enthusiasm on behalf of other people's possessions or good fortune; an enthusiasm quite untinged with envy.

"It suits you both, somehow. Just right for you," she said, as we stood on the terrace admiring the view, which was indeed showing its loveliest aspect with the autumn golds and reds and russets of the trees spread before us across the patchwork pattern of little English fields under a blue sky with puffy white clouds like sheep.

We showed her our plan for the garden, and she surprised us by some very good suggestions of her own, as well as some that sent Gareth's eyebrows soaring. She had overcome her first wary shyness with him, and they were on easy terms, so that she took his teasing in her stride. It was never unkind, though, for Gareth had sensitive antennae now, and we had both grown very fond of her.

She had come on enormously during the past year. Working very hard, she had emerged from the secretarial course with credit, and at the beginning of September had joined the permanent staff of the Danville Typing Service as secretary to Joyce, and I had good reports of her. I had made a point of seeing her regularly, on our own in town as a rule, to counteract the undermining influence of her mother. She had recently moved to a bed-sitting room in a house in Wimbledon owned by an elderly relative of Joyce's who was delighted to have a young person in the house. It was only at alternate week-ends that she went home, and already I could see how much better she was for it.

She was developing fast, I thought. Nothing could alter her plainness, but there was a charm in her expansive smile, and she had taken to dressing in a flamboyant style, perhaps out of a sort of defiance, which came off and set a stamp of individuality on her.

Just before it was time to go that evening, she leaned her elbows on the mantelpiece and studied the picture she had given me. She had been obviously delighted to see it there. Her mother had taken care to inform her that no picture would be worth hanging at the derisory price she had paid for it and it had taken me quite a time to make her believe that the picture hadn't been an embarrassment to me. Now it hung in the most prominent position in our sitting-room.

"You know, that really was a wonderful holiday, wasn't it?" she observed now. "I'll never forget it. Do you believe in fate?" she asked us.

"We-ell," I said cautiously. "Perhaps."

"Certainly," said Gareth firmly.

She smiled at him.

"So do I. That holiday was fateful. I mean, you go on, year after year, expecting something to happen and nothing does and you're still left with your miserable self. Then, when you least expect it, something does happen. Fate steps in and life's never the same again. A turning point. That's what it was for me. And it was sort of fateful for you, too, wasn't it?"

"Very fateful," I said, meeting the amused gaze of the architect of my fate sitting no more than a yard away.

"The very best thing that ever happened to me," said Ann, turning her gaze back to the mountain.

"My sentiments, too," I said. "That's why that picture is my dearest possession and it shall hang there until I die."

Ann flashed me a brilliant smile and Gareth stood up and rested a hand on my shoulder for a moment before saying:

"If we're to catch that train, we must be moving, Ann. I'll get the car round."

We drove her to the station, and she hung out of the train window waving to us until a curve in the line took her out of sight.

"Well, your ewe lamb is certainly growing up fast," said Gareth as we walked back to the car.

"But not losing her blessed simplicity."

It was only a short drive back to the house through narrow lanes fringed with fallen leaves. The car headlights picked up the silver trails of travellers' joy in the hedgerows. A slip of a new moon was visible above the trees ahead of us. The lantern in the porch and the house lights looked welcoming as we turned into the drive.

"It begins to feel like home," observed Gareth.

"I love it," I declared extravagantly, conscious of a need to express my gratitude to what Ann would call fate for the deep happiness I knew now.

> " 'I will make a palace fit for you and me
> Of green days in forests and blue days at sea.'

Remember, Kate?"

"That evening with Miss Courtland. Of course I remember. And I have my man to thank for the star-shine, too," I said, putting my hand on Gareth's as he stopped the car.

"I love you," he said, taking me in his arms. "Don't think I've said that for some time."

"We don't have to say it now that we live it. Except now and again, just for the record."

"Tonight, when you said it was the best thing that ever happened to you. Truly, Kate?"

"Do you need to ask?"

"Not really. The same goes for me, too. Our marriage is the best thing that ever happened to me. I knew it would be, of course. You were the one who took convincing."

"And how! Ann reminded me tonight. What a holiday that was!"

"You certainly indulged in some strange caperings."

"And you were too clever for me, as always."

"You know what the trouble was."

"Tell me, Solomon."

"It never entered your head that I could learn from experience, too. You just ran, like the Red Queen in Alice."

"You managed to put salt on my tail, for all that. I shall never know quite to what extent you had it all in hand from the word go."

He smiled and kissed me, then let me go, saying:

"It was a very tricky assignment, anyway. Let's leave it at that. And I don't intend to make love to you in the car when we've got a perfectly comfortable house awaiting us."

I left him to put the car away, and went to the sitting-room to collect some cups and glasses, but found myself studying the picture again. Sort of fateful, indeed. Looking back at my old panic-stricken self then, I seemed as far removed from that now as I was from the twenty-year-old who had run away. This year had been so rich in fulfilment. With our busy professional lives dove-tailed within the framework of our deepening love for each other, I could not envisage now the shallowness of my life without Gareth. When he was away on a job I felt his absence like an amputation, although I had work of my own to immerse myself in. Of course, there was no doubt who was the senior partner in our marriage, but it was a partnership, and we had found a happy balance, as

Gareth had predicted. And his hand on the reins was so gentle and subtle now that I found it comforting and had no disposition to rebel.

The picture of the mountain, with its glacier gleaming and sinister, and the chalet lower down where Ann had eaten the outsize Sachertorte, recalled it all so plainly. What an amazing mixture of farce and drama, tragedy and comedy, hostility and love, that holiday had been. Like Ann, I should never forget it. I might perhaps in time be vague about Miss Courtland, Monsieur Corbeil, Max Corinth; remember only dimly what it was like standing on that ledge in the relentless rain. But I should never forget tearing down that hill to the smashed Mercedes, fearing Gareth was dead; never forget the night in the hut nor the peace of those moments with Gareth when we saw the mountains spread out before us in the moonlight; and sharpest of all in its details, I should never, never forget that moment of time when I had sat at the table by the fountain and looked across the courtyard to see Gareth standing there, and had felt as though a bomb had exploded beneath me.